BLACK SCIENCE

by

WARREN FREEMAN

To order additional copies contact:

www.lulu.com

No   Weapon   That   Is
Formed   Against   Thee
Shall Prosper.

Isaiah 54:17

This novel was inspired by and is dedicated
to the tireless imagination of my
lovely wife Deborah.
-Thanks-

Foreword:

In the next ten years, if the past ten are any indication; we're all in for a crushing deluge of overwhelmingly shocking information hitting us harder and faster than we can gather it in and deal with it. The news headlines surely will, as usual, shock and frighten us and make many of us wish for a return to these here good old days. Those headlines will surely include the usual wars, calamities, disasters, terrorist activities, new diseases, and GOD knows what else.

This book speculates; with black scientists in the fore, science will soon unravel even more wondrous revelations than ever before dreamed of. One of them is producing actual truthful visions of the past, near and ancient; not what historians have sincerely but naively postulated, but the actual exhibiting of past historical occurrences in their live, precise, vivid entirety for mass consumption on your very own TV screen. Imagine watching the actual Sermon on the Mount, every bloody battle in history, or the ancient Egyptians using wind sails to erect their pyramids in real time, or the myriad carnivorous dinosaurs doing what they do best; eat each other; all right there on your own TV in screaming, blood curdling, uncensored reality as it is happening instead of second-hand as an animated fantasy. What changes will this undiluted surfeit of readily available past reality "bites" affect a world of people who can't face what little of the allowed truth they are privy to now?

Change will shape all of our lives, those that survive, hopefully for the better, but realistically that's a pipe dream. Many will suffer and die as we wrestle to live, love, learn, and maintain our all too tenuous foothold on this planet; a foothold that some are at this very moment pulling out from under us all in the name of outrageous profit. Thus warned, I hope you readers are enlightened and amused and able to benefit in some way from the following pages as I was.

F.S.S.

"- Sir Boss -

To be sure, I'm still down on whores.

Though now-a-days, I'll rip them and most anybody else too!"

-Jack-2016-

Chapter 1

Thursday, September 29, 2016

Dave Asher uneasily settled himself back into his second ever in life first class; quite cushy seat, and nervously awaited the lift off. The large, hulking, bald, deep ebony toned Bruno Guntz; vested company bodyguard and reluctant valet, sat ostensibly coolly and quietly at his right side. With eyes shut tight in dread, and facing straight ahead, Bruno's large, bare, shining flat dome was illuminated smoothly by the soft orange hued overhead lights.

Dave peered out the passenger jet's port side window, under the heavy, gray, cloud cover, up at the surrealistically contrived, imposing, steel structures of the eastern disk and wondered if the lift off would be as exhilarating as the ascent a few days ago had been.

Earlier this week in the early fall chill of September 2016 the jump jet had flew roaring in eastward from Chicago dramatically circling around the disk. Dave was aboard; in coach, returning sooner than he had expected from his assignment where he'd "caught" some particularly gruesome gangland shootings from the thirties. His short layover in New York had proven to be shorter than expected, thus this trip.

The disk; a three storied, mile long, circle of steel and cement sat heavily, majestically, square atop the six individual, one hundred and twenty storied towers of the new World Trade Center.

After two turns around the disk the jet nestled above its landing pad, and abruptly lifted its front forty five degrees above its horizontal axis. This maneuver rudely pushed the passengers back into their seats and vertically lifted them precariously up and onto their backs as the jet slid backwards and down on it's own belly and rear for it's harrowingly ostentatious showy landing.

The experience had frightened some and excited others. Dave hated to admit it but he had inadvertently fallen into the former group even though the maneuver had been well anticipated by all including him.

Suddenly, violently, the vertical take off passenger jump jet forcefully revved its engines to an almost painfully screaming loud pitch and crouched, then lurched once and smoothly jumped up off the pad as a cat might in one fell motion.

Dave felt the pressurized cabin suddenly squeeze his eyes together as his rear was pushed down in his seat as the craft forcefully but slowly, inexorably gained altitude through the sheer brute strength of its turbine fusion engines. As the jet cleared the disk's massive bulk Dave had occasion to see the craggy New York skyline in dark outline below in the late evening setting Sun's dying glow through gathering dark cumulus storm clouds from out his porthole window.

Bruno remained sitting stoically passive and Dave whimsically wondered for a moment if the giant still lived.

Below, on the Brooklyn side, Dave caught sight of the fifty-storied, metal latticed, Tesla tower rising out of the almost totally abandoned slums as the silver jet now swung east. The Tesla tower, the very first of the hundred so far completed was the bold defiant initiative by the Cresasern group. It exuded a piercingly bright red glow from its topmost spire as the evening Sun fell. The tower spat out into the atmosphere, as readily evidenced by its reddish pulsing spire topping out at three hundred feet up, free power to the masses fueled by a massive nuclear plant below ground. It was the ultimate in Wi-Fi technology; wireless energy transmission. The initiative was bold, and dangerous, because it flew in the face of the vested energy interests and protests from the established fossil fuel energy combines who still wanted things to remain the same as in the last century when they enjoyed a monopoly on pricing, resources, and distribution control. All one now needed was a one hundred dollar receptacle; a "Clowder", they called it, leased by Cresasern, or one of their affiliated concerns and you had free unlimited energy use. Simply plug the devices into your easily modified car or whatever appliance you wished and it would run them free of ongoing oil cartel rapidly rising charges.

For once in its history, the human race enjoyed a surfeit of cheap unlimited energy and each once all powerful oil concern's camp warred against the other for rapidly dwindling market share. The newly cash flow poor O.P.E.C. countries didn't like it one whit. But as a happy consequence of this shift away from the world's dependence on the rapidly drying up fossil fuel fields in their countries was also a drastic shift of the world's simmering greed induced wars and bloody hotspots away from their homes and backyards. Now with the western bloc's meddling gone all O.P.E.C. had left was their own frequent bloody in-house wars between their own once rich oil barons whipping up the little people. Those same little people, you know, the ones that never shared in the oil loot, whipped up against each other, Dave noted sadly.

Of course, if the misguided U.S. governmental administration in D.C.; through gross misfeasance and malfeasance, hadn't bankrupted their very own country politically and economically, and seriously endangered the world's environment to the point of civil civic intervention in

2007 none of this would've happened, Dave surmised, reminiscing.

Many changes were forcefully forced on all; including the radically draconian Congressional measure to curtail capitalism's greed by limiting oil company profits to 200%. For once the fox watching the hen house did a good job, if only to save their own hides. No longer on the back burner; the need to rapidly change energy sources from the use of polluters to non polluters, and invent Earth environmental saving processes, now not later, rudely slapped the world in its face.

Dave marveled that the world's old-line cash-starved energy monopolies hadn't already blown up the impudent competitor upstart's tower. The Cresasern Group weren't altruistic fools though, Dave gathered from news reports. The free energy use was for one year only. After that you would have to pay a fee, albeit one much smaller than the almost quarterly ever rising fees that had been routinely charged by the once all-powerful oil monopolies, but an ongoing fee nonetheless for the leasing of their "Clowder" receptacles.

The pollution free energy spire forcefully radiated its shimmering red spines out into the quickly falling dark blanket of the night as the 10:00 P.M. Red-eye jet swiftly left the U.S. eastern seaboard and climbing, headed up to above forty thousand feet for its three hour trip to London.

The long telescoping steel handcuff chain tugged at Dave's left wrist reminding him of the precious cargo attached to him. The thick black leather briefcase sat between his feet beckoning loudly to him with a noisily strident message of such a distastefully singular purpose that Dave hadn't had the initiative or inclination to listen to in many years.

"Nice take off," Bruno rumbled in his deep ominous baritone, his large dark brown eyes opening wide at last and darting nervously to and fro.

"It talks?" chided Dave. "Found your balls have you? It's nice to finally have you aboard."

He would good-naturedly bully the giant from now until they touched down, but not too much; not truly mean-spirited. Just enough to take the giant's mind off the fact that he was suspended in a gas-filled tube with small wings far up in the air somewhere where he didn't really care to be at all.

Bruno was usually even-tempered but he wasn't that nice a guy. Nor was he a friend, for as Bruno oft said gruffly: "I got no friends!"

Dave had worked with Bruno once before but still knew little of the glum fellow. Little that is except that he came from a large, poor, single parent household from a slum, thus his terse, cloudy, take on life was most understandable.

The video-screen button on the back of the seat in front of Dave blinked red announcing an incoming call.

Dave pressed the red light and at once a one by one square foot hologram appeared suspended before him. The face and upper torso of Olivia Takahaski appeared though barely swathed in a bright red "V" scalloped bulging breast-revealing dress. Her overly large, dark black oval eyes sparkled mischievously within her pretty pert heart-shaped face.

Dave grabbed the outer edges of the hologram and pulled outwards and up until the hologram was twice as large as in its original form.

"Ziv asked me to call," she sexily cooed with her full pouting red lips sensuously beckoning, as she was consciously, overtly, bending over to afford Dave a better view of her pretty new, well-oiled bulging almond hued orbs.

"You do have all your papers? We wouldn't want a repeat of last year's Balkan debacle," she continued with black flashing eyes a fluttering wildly.

Dave winced. Last year the Croats had confiscated his device and remanded him for a month in Slovensky Prison until they themselves had lazily tired of running their red tape all over him.

Behind her Dave spied a few dual fanjet-powered flying buzz cabs flitting about amongst the storm cloudy New York City skyline.

"Yes honey I'm all set," Dave sneered, thinking; Damn! She is good looking! But, Ziv Finkel, big time CEO of Image Retrieval Inc. wouldn't bother himself with such mundane detail. No he slyly concluded; she was calling on her own to make sure he was on this flight.

He figured that by tonight there'd be another man in her bed, probably that slimy elf Rolf Schneider from public relations. Yes Rolf' would definitely be a social step up for her from a lowly "catcher". One good thing Dave guiltily thought: his wallet would swell once again without her high maintenance demands put upon it while his member cried foul in useless defiance.

Bruno started evidencing signs of life and slyly gawked over at her obvious bulging cleavage hanging out of the hologram with his naturally obvious lecherous eyes.

Olivia suggestively tongued her pen and ignoring Bruno's stare smiled at Dave and sternly ordered, "keep us appraised of your progress daily and don't do anything blatantly illegal! You hear---?"

"What isn't illegal except dope in England, especially the Extraminator? I'll have to wear a muzzle the entire time I'm there and they've already said they're gonna assign some watchdog to watch over us so we don't uncover and reveal any state secrets. Couldn't someone else have gone instead of me?" Dave childishly groused.

She absently-mindedly tugged at her scalloped bodice almost freeing her barely confined but straining to be set free honey hued breasts.

"Stop whining Dave, you need a career boost. You might, if you stop wasting time crying, have a nice time. Well, I got to go. See ya love," Olivia said tersely, quickly clicking off.

Dave was left staring at the fuzzy blank screen as he mouthed the words to thin air and the muffled smirk of Bruno, "see you too love."

Bruno mockingly gazed at Dave with a feigned hound dog droop to his big brown eyes.

Dave felt the pounding in his head and heart and knew his blood pressure was rising. Though his doctor said it was impossible he could swear that he felt the many genetically engineered minute nannites in his blood stream chew up his excess LDL cholesterol all the faster even as his heart pumped stronger.

"Don't even try it! I can take it. A job is a job, and as long as I'm working I'm getting paid. That's all there is to it. She ain't all that to me anyway!" Dave said angrily slamming his hand into the red button, abruptly terminating the cohesion of the fuzzy screen.

The rest of the flight was spent in cold civil silence by Dave and the effects of air fear by Bruno until the robotic food servers arrived and the warmed over cardboard serving as their meal thawed out the atmosphere somewhat.

Olivia had been right though. Dave knew all too well that he badly needed a career boost.

The rotund personage of Cecil Bliven as usual came painfully to mind as Dave's paranoia took on a physical shape in his mind. Bliven; head sales manager at Sweetgood heating and cooling, gave physical body to Dave's present nagging fears and insecurities. Bliven, after somehow having stuffed his unevenly brown skinned potato shaped, overweight, form into a lime green suit two sizes too small peered out over his wire rims. He said with much authority, "Mister Asher, I see you completed your required military service, and you received a three point seven average in college. Your results on our aptitude test are very good, but, I hate to tell you this---. You're just too smart for us! I'm sorry but we can't use you...!"

Bliven spoke this evenly with a straight pudgy face, punctuating his remarks with a holo-graph indeed showing Dave's measured intellect in a red line soaring far above the blue lined median scores of the slavishly toiling sales staff just outside Bliven's office.

Dave had heard many odd things in his life, especially of late as he job-hunted, but this was a first. Not the usual from the man: "No experience, we'll call you..." Or: "No openings presently." But: "Too smart for a job...!" Dave's stomach had turned as the words assaulted his ears. It was always something, no matter what the reason, big or small; in the end Dave didn't get hired. Strangely he had become resigned to it by now. But this reason was a novel first, coming from a brother no less, and it still hurtfully stuck in his mind as though a large hot iron shaft had been forcefully wedged into and through his skull straight into his brain. That day Dave nervously laughed insanely, he hoped; to himself only; all the way home on the monorail.

After seven bleak months of his searching to no avail Image Retrieval responded with an offer, a small offer to be sure, but his first. Dave jumped at it. He had to; he was broke. The offered job of "catcher" sat two steps above secretarial but had the perks of travel, adventure, and better pay.

Still, the whys and unanswered wherefores of this and all assignments from this company nagged him, especially now. Foremost: Why did the BBC need him, li'l old Dave the catcher, to bring over an L.D.E.? Even though the devices were illegal in England he knew they had plenty of them and professionals to use them stashed away. Everybody knew the BBC was above the mundane people's law, so what's the sweat? What the hell is this shit really all about? It didn't make any sense at all to him and Dave knew from experience that that meant that his ass would be left out to dry somehow someway soon for sure.

After a while Bruno grunted and nudged Dave, awaking him from his troubled reverie.

"Land ho!" Bruno grunted.

Following Bruno's intrusive massive arm and large pointing hand Dave peered through the overhead cloud cover and saw below New Heathrow airport jutting out into the choppy gray Atlantic Ocean from the east English port city of South End on Sea. The international entry only airport sat alone on a ten-mile man made peninsula rudely jutting out from the British shore into the sea.

The jump jet banked hard and rolled over on its side as it cleaved through the buffeting, heavy gray clouds on its downward spiral.

Later, after their usual harrowing landing, the many overhead, silver hued, oval airborne buzzers busily flew about and buzzed this way and that. They avidly shone their yellow and red lasers down onto the passengers moving on the tram below. Every now and again one would dip down to eye level, shoot its lights onto a passenger then chirp once or twice and rapidly regain altitude. All this was very disconcerting, especially to Dave.

As the tram pulled them toward a big sign reading: "Examination"; Dave was accosted by not one but two flying buzzers at once. They hung about him a bit too long for his liking and chirped away, then left as abruptly as they had arrived.

"They sure do got the hots for you," Bruno laughed in his slow East Jersey City street vernacular with a wide grin borne more out of relief at being on the ground than malice while easily shouldering their overnight bags.

Dave shrugged and felt the weight of his shackled package grip him tighter around his right wrist.

The packed crowd on the tram moved on mostly in sullen silence and fear. Some, the veterans, knew what awaited them at "Examination's" reception, some didn't, but all were apprehensive.

Soon Dave and Bruno found themselves in a very large domed lobby and all went about seeking the proper line to get in. Above and emblazoned was signs noting countries of origin. Dave and Bruno both lined up at the end of the "United States" line.

Then for the first time Dave noticed them. They walked slowly, solemnly, in pairs and in threes dressed all in black shiny body armor and high boots with big, ugly, automatic weapons at the ready. Dave took them for special police of some unknown type by their shiny helmets, white belts, and white sashes. Pulled-down visors ominously and dramatically shielded their faces and they wore large lighted medallions on their chests that Dave surmised were detection devices of some kind. Three of them soon surrounded a nattily dressed tall pallid-complexioned white-haired man sitting on a bench against the wall across from Dave. The man looked up at them with just a twist of a wan smile etched on his old craggy pale face.

The buzzers having already singled out the man now retreated back upward to watch over the crowd. Sullenly the nervous crowd watched the enfolding tableau with rapt attention. The man shakily stood as he was bade to do and began answering questions. Dave couldn't hear what they were saying but still he watched the enfolding drama as avidly as did all the other arrivals.

Suddenly the first policeman's device blinked on and turned green. The second's turned yellow, and as the third's turned red the tall man bolted away and ran. He ran right toward the waiting line and bumped right into Dave with his arms outstretched.

For a second their frightened eyes met and Dave felt all too sharply the other fellow's pain.

"Zither81," whispered the distraught man as he grasped Dave's lapels tightly, desperately.

With their upset eyes locked, Dave suddenly discerned the man's eyes soften and his pain ebb a bit as he untangled himself and ran anew this time down the long waiting line toward the exit. He didn't get far though, as the stalking trio coolly cut loose on him with their all too ready firearms. The fellow got about four feet before he yelled and abruptly stopped and fell in a heap on the floor, neatly riddled through his back.

Dave and Bruno hit the ground at the loud sounds of the gunfire only to find to their confusion and embarrassment that they were the only ones so severely affected. The rest of the crowd barely blinked an eye.

Rising, Dave and Bruno sheepishly smiled at each other as the somber murderous trio now eyed them suspiciously and started over their way. Quickly surrounding Dave and Bruno they glowered menacingly as one burly fellow wasted no time in sticking his gun rudely into Bruno's oversize gut and shouted, "Get back!"

Bruno eagerly complied as sweat formed on his massive brow.

"You know that bloke?" barked another highly agitated fellow, referring to the dead man with a callous wave of his gun.

"No," Dave answered quickly.

"What did he say to you?" quizzed the nervous officer, getting closer to Dave. Pulling up his visor revealed the man's menacing face. A large red nose, cold sneer, and steel blue eyes amid his unnaturally contorted features rudely greeted Dave. The man pushed his grim face no more than six inches away from Dave's and Dave felt the man's hot tepid breath fuel his own growing nervous concern.

"Nothing," Dave lied, convincingly, he hoped.

"What you got there sport...? Some Black Science it appears!" evilly barked the all too close fellow now tormenting Dave with a rude nudge of his gun into Dave's ribs, referring to Dave's package. The fact that the guard's light lit up green punctuated severely Dave's growing sense of dread.

"Black Science---!" the guard sneered again.

The mere mention of that term caused Dave to shudder in fear, for he knew from experience what usually followed when a white man with a gun said that. Not smiles and cold brews, oh no, not that.

One other officer's blinker turned red, another's turned yellow and Dave knew the shit was about to hit the fan.

"I got a permit from the BBC and the government!" Dave wailed then stammered again, sweating profusely as he nervously dug in his pockets for said lifeline. Bruno tensed himself for some quick but probably futile action.

The menacing black clad trio tensed for the expected fight or flight from their victims that they were woefully used to by now and readied their guns.

"Hold on!" suddenly boomed loudly from behind Dave and Bruno. "Those chickens are mine!"

The order came, as Dave turned to see, from a smallish, slim young woman clad in form hugging well tailored black leather. Her close cropped reddish-black hair framed large sparkling almond hued eyes in a field of smooth ochre toned skin. Her full red lips snarled the order much louder than her small frame should have allowed, Dave thought very surprised. She was flanked by her muscle: two hulking dark green clad BBC guards holding their large "crunchers" aimed square on the trio of police giving Dave and Bruno the business.

"Stand down wankers, or I'll have my boys crunch you!" she barked most authoritatively, in a tone belying the fact that she routinely was used to giving orders.

The policemen shrank back and obviously knowing her and her bigger friends left with no lip, just a backward sneer and little else.

"Th---Thanks," Dave stammered.

"Heda Marish, BBC, and you must be Dave Asher and friend," she said curtly, holding up her shiny gold identity badge.

"Is that it? Is it fully functioning?" she asked coldly, now gesturing toward Dave's shackled cargo.

Dave could only shake his head in the affirmative, now distracted by her pleasing form and mesmerized by the large size of her guard's weapons.

"Good, we're behind schedule, follow me!" she curtly barked and turned briskly on her heel.

Within the hour they were in the underground bullet tube train running from South End on Sea north into London in a private car. Heda sat comfortably between her two burly friends as Dave and Bruno sat opposite on the other bench of the private car. All the while she avidly conversed while using her swivel eyepiece over her right eye in some unheard of before, to Dave, vernacular of speedy Cockney into her headset while busily tapping about on her omni-pad, without giving him or Bruno nary a passing glance.

The guards sat stoically, quietly cradling their large silver-black tubes or "crunchers" as they were called. The weapons shot out compressed sound waves in an electrically charged ball of air and would knock you down if you didn't resist the force of the blast. If you did resist it would surely break some of your bones and still knock you down. They also, like Heda, had automatic laser pistols strapped on their hips for insurance and it didn't escape Dave's notice that both guards were more so covering Bruno and not him. From the scowl on Bruno's face that fact wasn't lost on him also.

"Here, you'll use our disk only in that device of yours!" She instructed curtly, unlocking the handcuff and case shackled to Dave's wrist and thrusting said silver toned DVD at him.

Dave silently proceeded to extract the encased device and load the BBC disk as ordered.

He wasn't sure he liked her at all. She looked good enough; black leather clad shapely legs crossed pertly, real nice figure, and nice heart shaped face too. No he just didn't feel that there was enough information to form an opinion as to her character. Her real personality she hid well, he figured, that is if she had one. No, as more time passed, he was pretty sure he didn't like her.

Thus vexed, Dave spent his time idly watching the passing English rolling countryside all green and smooth and occasionally; Heda. He wondered who she was and where did she come from. He finally surmised that she was a mixture of New Delhi and Haitian stock though he wasn't at all sure he was right.

Heda's ample, soft feminine curves nestling fetchingly across from him caused Dave to play the "what if" game in his racing mind. What if they were an item? What if she actually went for his tired line? Would their relationship be bliss, or horror? Dave wondered on about what it would be like; refreshing, or a painful time? Most women he had been involved with had at least waited until they had their hooks deep in him to show him what they were really about, unlike this one that screamed "witch" straightaway from the get go. Dave was totally perplexed by her, but still interested.

The hour long boring ride didn't elicit one iota of polite conversation from all concerned.

Soon they were in London and quickly bustled by land cab through the heavily fogged, dark city to their still unknown, to Dave, destination deep in Whitechapel. The cab sped east past Big Ben, over London Bridge, and on by Trafalgar Square fast, way too fast for Dave to enjoy any of his much overdue and highly anticipated vacation destinations.

Dave noticed that the storm from New York had seemingly followed them here as evidenced by the cold foggy rain and drizzle overcast. He also noted that London's new silver skyscrapers jutting up into the clouds seemed at war with the older architecture which wasn't moving out without a fight. The terrorist bombings of 2008 had left plenty of free space and now both styles warred for dominance.

Checking his watch, he found it showed; 3:00A.M. New York time; 8:00 A.M. London time. Damn, no wonder he was tired, he thought.

Arriving at their as yet unspecified destination, Heda turned Dave over to the director Sam Wellsey who wasted little time with introductions and curtly filled Dave in on the particulars of his assignment. The gruff, gray haired wiry fellow, foppishly dressed in tan colored baggy bamboo plant derived faux-tweeds, exuded much false pomposity; actually more out of habit than actual prowess, but he was blissfully unaware of it.

"You're On Berner Street, number 40, near Duffield's Yard, where on Saturday September 30, 1888 at around 1:00A.M., the body of Elizabeth Stride was found dead, ostensibly sliced ear to ear by Jack The Ripper. It is postulated that he was prematurely disturbed in his work here because she wasn't as badly sliced as was his usual M.O.... Also over on Mitre Square the body of Catherine Eddowes was found later around 1:45 A.M. that very same night. That'll be our second shot to do tonight. Got that?"

"Sure I got it." Dave answered tersely, becoming quite annoyed by being pushed around by the usual everyday brusque rudeness of his hosts.

The rain had finally ceased and now all that remained was the wet chill and the heavy swirling fog. The fog hung heavy like a wool robe over the street as it gave the street lights an ominous hazy aura that caused Dave to shiver in unease.

"Can you calibrate that thing for about 12:30 A.M. or so on the night in question, right there, ground zero as it were?" Wellsey asked, snidely pointing a long thin crooked finger to a particular section of the street pavement marked with a chalk "X".

Dave nodded, now noticing the growing crowd of locals massing quickly behind the police barricades. His unease grew.

Heda, her guards, and Bruno stood back wisely.

"Then do it, let's "catch" this now, and get this show on the road!" Wellsey snorted, "We'd like to air tomorrow night!"

It didn't take Dave long to set up. Popping out his tripod and mounting and adjusting his device's settings were pure child's play by now for him. Soon the area along the street in question was illuminated by the eerie initial blue glow of the Extraminator at work.

The Extraminator; the much improved successor to the Light Discernment Extraroseter, or L.D.E. as it was called by industry insiders, illuminated the past. No larger than a camcorder, it expertly sifted through seemingly long gone light wave images of the past and putting them back together in their originality; producing a holographic image of any event that happened recently or way back long ago.

All at once the Extraminator shot out three beams of red, yellow, and blue light which crisscrossed themselves in a wide swinging to and fro arc, then with a loud clap, congealed together and produced a six foot by six foot square holographic image of that dark sad night long ago right over the area designated as ground zero.

Dave still never ceased to get a whole body invigorating rush from this abrupt opening of a gateway to the past right from out of the seemingly nothingness of thin air.

The uneasy crowd shuffled for position nervously and avidly swiveled their heads to see the image unfolding.

"More light! I need more light on the image!" Dave implored.

Wellsey bade his anxious assistant; Ruth, a tall, thin, nervous woman; shine more light on the unfolding image. She gamely huffed and puffed and pulled over a large floodlight on a wheeled pole to illuminate the square image.

With that done figures started to become legible in the shimmering hologram. A woman, tall, gaunt and haggard in appearance appeared pacing about and then she greeted an approaching man. He was well dressed sporting a beaver skinned bowler hat and carrying a square black bag. Without much ado, just a look about behind him, or conversing he produced a long shiny knife from his bag and slashed across her neck with one fast clean stroke and she fell down immediately clutching her neck. He bent down towards her prone body; blood dripping knife now raised high.

The crowd erupted in a series of loud groans and then shouts of anger, fright, and fear.

"More light!" Dave bellowed loudly, bravely, though now quite frightened himself.

The harried assistant shakily rushed over and brought over another floodlight.

On the square "screen" the "Ripper" stopped abruptly at this time and looking straight out in Dave's direction seemed to regard intently the hologram itself as well as all the people assembled to watch him and his crime some one hundred twenty eight years later, in the future.

The Ripper's face that looked back over time was maliciously contorted. Every wrinkle exuded his evil intent. Hatred radiated from him strongly especially through his bright red eyes and gaunt mustachioed menacing features. His teeth glinted like a tiger's. The man looked for all like a devil caught in the unholy throes of some unwholesome excitement. His long square nose's nostrils flared so wide that Dave fully expected smoke to issue from them at any moment.

Dave felt a real sharp shiver of fear slide fast down his back to his butt.

Beholding this horrible apparition staring back at them; the crowd suddenly screamed in terror, broke through the police barricades and started to run in panic this way and that, any way that they hoped was far away.

The assistant screamed also and being pushed herself; knocked over the lights. Amid the exploding, sparking, and flashing, crashing lights, the hologram screen went suddenly blank and confusion, fear, and blind terrifying panic reigned that night on Berner Street.

Dave and the L.D.E. setup were knocked over by the rush of escaping humanity and as he shakily rose he saw the impossible. A tall darkly dressed man in a bowler with requisite black bag ran seemingly from right out of the hologram screen and swiftly slashed the assistant across her neck and then proceeded to run among and in with the crowd slashing away at the fleeing people as they ran.

Dave watched; struck dumfounded as the "slasher" and crowd all disappeared around a corner until all that was left on Berner Street this night was a bloody body here and there writhing in pain under a cloud of thick fear and Dave could swear that he heard the plaintive cry of a wolf howling out into the night!

Chapter 2

Saturday, October 1, 2016

The shiny brushed metal door's gold placard read: "F.E. Albion Chief Inspector Homicide."

Dave had quietly waited in the bustling corridor and inwardly, nervously, watched mostly the passing throng of cops and criminals and of course, the sign for the past two hours as Heda, Bruno, Wellsey, and even the BBC guards had each been summoned in.

The cold-blooded shooting of that man at the airport and the bloody mayhem on Berner Street had taken its toll on Dave's nerves and sanity. Two nights of restless half-sleep had frayed his raw nerves to the breaking point also. It appeared that his premonition of bad times ahead was becoming all too true. And what was up with the term "Zither81", he wondered?

Dave didn't fault the British their draconian ways, oh no. They had long, too long, borne the brunt of the war on terrorism with its plethora of bombings, killings, and everyday gas attacks so often that now once guaranteed civil trials, were suspended in lieu of summary executions once you were branded a terrorist, and thus everyone's civil rights had decidedly suffered. To their credit the British had realized before many other countries that the world was in the midst of a very hot third world war; albeit one of an overtly religious nature.

This morning they had all been bustled into cubicles and asked questions in a very rude demeanor in a droll female voice by a small round pod sitting ominously in the center of the desk. The results of the interviews printed out on a silver metallic paper titled "Statement" which Dave promptly rolled up and inserted into his jacket pocket and he waited.

Waiting didn't bother him, hell; he was well used to waiting. Three unsuccessful foster care placements had earned him a permanent bed at Saint Mary's orphanage in Yeadon Pennsylvania; waiting. Waiting patiently, even hopelessly, in the orphanage while all the other kids got adopted sooner or later, and not he had slowly ingrained a hard grit into his backbone. That grit now served him well in dealing with the myriad bad hands life dealt us all and him in particular. Problem was; that hard core grit worked so well it efficiently and effectively cut him off from seeing and capitalizing on any good that naively wandered his way, Dave knew. To counter that he now daily prayed to GOD that his mind balance itself to steer himself a somewhat more rational, honorable, course through life than his cold, hard, experiences would more naturally dictate that he follow.

Now finally it was his turn. Heda exited without even a glance his way as a young uniformed copper opened the door and beckoned him in.

The room appeared to be in a time warp, an old, waist high, wooden cased radio sat dustily over in a corner. There were old pictures pasted all over on the walls and there was even a fireplace on the far wall that Dave knew couldn't be real.

Inside the room sat a tall, portly, pale, balding man behind a large mahogany desk. His face had long ago lost its chiseled male definition and now sadly hung in many loose, sagging, folds around his jowls. The large man absent-mindedly tugged at his suspenders holding up his all the rage now faux-tweed tan trousers.

The young copper stayed and stood nearby; his pistol all too obvious at the ready perched high on his left hip.

Behind the balding man hung an old, large one dimensional TV screen. Its sound was muted but the messages appeared in printed white text at the bottom saying: "Rioting continues in Marseilles!....Moslems retake Chechnya capital!....House of Saud falls to democratic coup, Bushes flee back to U.S.!....Positron Engine Driven Dauntless probe to Saturn's moon Enceladus returning with supposedly live specimens aboard!"

The head man busily scribbled in what appeared to be a real paper filled ledger book, while consulting a liquid PC notebook. He quickly looked up but once and bade Dave take the chair facing the desk.

"Statement!" Albion barked gruffly, thrusting out a nervously shaking outstretched arthritic right hand.

Dave complied and watched as the man seriously perused the silvered paper Dave had proffered then began jotting in his ledger anew. At last Albion stopped and placed the ledger aside and regarded Dave solemnly with blood shot green eyes. The man seriously chewed doggedly at something in his mouth just as he appeared to be chewing on Dave's involvement in the matter at hand.

"It appears that all interviewed agree on the terrible events of two nights ago up to a point. Interestingly half of those interviewed diverge when it comes to where this fellow, the perpetrator, came from. Oddly, no one, including you, can supply me with a definitive description of him. Some say he came from the crowd, some say he jumped right out of your created hologram," Albion snorted, swallowing whatever cud he had been chewing, all the while eyeing Dave hungrily, seemingly as the target of his next meal.

"You on the other hand are amazingly hazy on that particular point. Why?" Albion asked smugly.

"I was face down on the ground and dazed. I didn't have a good field of vision, but I'm sure he didn't come out of the hologram. He had to come from the crowd," Dave stammered.

"Dave Asher..? Right..? Catcher for only a little over a year...? You're low man on the seniority totem pole? Right...? What gift gives you the professional expertise to come to that conclusion?" Albion snickered haughtily slowly starting to turn red in the face.

The young copper snickered also but not as openly.

"There's never been an instance of the hologram acting as a time portal in the ten years it's been in use. It's physically and scientifically impossible for the hologram to be anything but a mirror on the past," Dave bravely stated from memory, Image Retrieval's manuals, and his training course.

Albion guffawed at this, the laugh originating deep in his bulbous belly.

"They told you that crap in catcher school? And you believed it?" Albion continued to laugh. The young copper now also openly snickered, mimicking his boss.

"Give me three minutes at the site with the Extraminator and I'll clear up that particular mystery," Dave said confidently.

"Not a chance sport, we've confiscated your device. We're analyzing its memory disk," Albion snidely sneered, rising and slamming his hands hard down on his desk for effect.

"You can't do that, its private property!" Dave answered back, quite surprised at his own temerity.

"King's property for the time being! The eggheads over at the Ministry of Information confiscated it, nicked it, they did, right out of me hand before I got a chance to look at it meself even. I imagine that it will be returned to you on

Monday morning when you fly home," Albion snorted angrily in his native Welsh brogue.

Dave now became quite disconcerted and felt the hot sweat start to run down his back in thick drops.

"I've got two dead people, five more critical, and you come in here with that "Black Science" drivel sonny. You "people" create this damn evil then loose it on the unsuspecting British public; mostly us white folk I may add, willy-nilly where I have to clean it up while you "boys" slink back on home. Have you seen the papers?" Albion snarled, angrily throwing the London dailies at Dave.

Taken aback Dave rose to his feet, his own anger boiling up in answer to Albion's overtly racial remarks.

The papers' headlines were inflammatory at the least, inciting riot; quite possible.

"Black Science Unleashes Demon!" "Jack The Ripper Walks The Streets Again Thanks To Black Yank Device!" "Panic Reigns as Jack Slashes Anew!" they loudly proclaimed.

"In your own country the divorce rate has tripled! Your jails are bursting with politicians, priests, and businessmen, --- and depression is rampant among a population that never could handle the truth before! "Black Science" has done all that. Can you deny it?" Albion asked smugly smiling.

"First off, I'm not a damn boy! Second: "Black Science" as you call it has saved this planet from a slow, hot death from greenhouse pollution and put money in your pocket! Money your oil cartel capitalist brothers were stealing from you happily. Your petrol prices have never been so low. And---in America we have the actual guilty criminals in jail, can you folks say that?" Dave shouted back feeling the back of his neck heat up.

"Over there we don't hamstring the police by limiting technology that might expose the power structure's crimes as well as the criminals' crimes! Perhaps its time we all faced the truth. I've used the Extraminator all over the globe and I still say it can't transport a man, or anything else, through time, it's still impossible," Dave continued angrily, turning to leave.

"Hold on a moment and tell me something master catcher?" Albion barked amusedly.

The young copper, stiff-armed, held Dave at the door, just long enough.

"Have you ever turned that machine on with the express intent to see a demon at work? Not a man, mind you, but a real demon as the press has called it, perhaps straight from hell? You do believe in hell don't you? It says it right here," Albion asked snidely, perusing his ledger.

Dave smiled back and said solemnly, "I sure do!" as he roughly pushed by the young guard.

~~~~~

Albion sat back down heavily, very pleased with himself. All his life he had considered himself a provoker. Even as a child he had prodded the other kids with words, sticks, and other ready instruments even, just to gage their reactions. Moreover, due to his pranks he learned a bit here and there, but also he ended up in detention more often than he cared to remember.

In adulthood his obtusely singular interest had grown to a skill, and now as an inspector in New Scotland Yard his talent had blossomed for the past thirty five years into a productive tool. He was quite happy by the way he had provoked the lad with racial sentiment and prejudice.

Albion knew that the average person, when angered sufficiently, would inadvertently give out more quantity and far more truthful information than you would have gotten from them by simply asking them nicely.

To the lad's credit he had responded back with facts, not fiction. Albion liked the kid's spunk. Albion didn't necessarily agree or disagree with Dave; he didn't feel the lad was an expert on the subject in question. Still, Albion knew all too well the miracles of modern science as evidenced both by the genetically engineered liver residing inside himself and the hard working scientific device attached to his own failing heart enabling him to live on borrowed time; five years so far.

Who knows what all is possible? Albion certainly knew he didn't know all and, as was his practiced habit, he would wait for more information to come; that is if the all-mighty Ministry of Information let him in on anything for once, in order to form a proper conclusion.

Perhaps the lad would be proven right in the end; that the ripper was a man of today, not a demon from yesterday, but Albion's policeman's mind would remain open for now on that subject, though personally he didn't believe in demons.

A knock on his door brought in another young cop with a note.

"We've found a copy of this on the body we just discovered in Whitechapel. The actual is down in forensics, it's addressed to you," said the fellow nervously.

With trembling fingers Albion opened the folded letter inwardly dreading what he knew in his gut and from thirty five years of dreary experience must be coming. It read in a twisted red scrawl that Albion knew from experience would prove to be in someone's blood:

"October 1, 2016,

Sir Boss, thanks for the lift. I don't quite understand how it was done but I'll try my best to fit in here. To be sure, I'm still down on whores. Though now-a days I'll rip them and most anybody else too! All because you interrupted me I'll have to start all over again. Bear with me as I'm trying my best. I took me a souvenir from this chap. Worry not there'll be more. I'll be in touch.

----Jack-----"

"Get my car! Quick---!", barked Albion as he rose to grab his coat, all the while crumpling the note in disgust in his large, twisted, right hand.

Behind him the video screen typed out: "Lost 1960's era A-bomb explodes 25 miles off the Savannah coast!....U.N. Headquarters in Beijing rocked by explosions!.... Large cavern discovered under Sphinx M.R.I'd; large oval object indicated!...Poor classes' begin another violent economic riot in Detroit and New York protesting low legal wage!"

~~~~~

Dave slowly walked down the building's long steep steps, still steaming inside, nursing a thorough dislike of Albion, totally convinced that the bigoted man had unresolved racial issues. He met Bruno and Heda and her armed entourage waiting at the step's base, outside New Scotland Yard on Broadway. None of them were smiling at all.

"What's wrong?" Dave asked naively.

"Your sightseeing trip is cancelled due to security issues," Heda reported coolly.

Not overly surprised at another usual negative Dave simply shrugged.

"We're ordered to escort you two back to the Carleton Arms where you'll stay incognito until Monday. There's just too much civil unrest in the city to ignore," Heda warned, hailing a passing land cab.

The cabbie took a long, hard, suspicious look at them and quickly passed on by.

"There's a double-decker, lets take it," Dave advised, pointing up the corner at a tall red open top bus; an ancient tourist attraction.

Soon they were boarding the red open-air bus and heading up its stairs for the top tier. Once seated, they sat back to enjoy the ride. The bus peacefully and leisurely ambled up Broadway for a while turned this way and that, and somewhat later turned onto Goodge Street and ran right into a growing waiting mob massing ahead.

Skinheads and neo-Nazis crowded into the street seemingly waiting for the bus, yelling unintelligible obscenities. Ugly, poorly dressed, young white men stood snarling, waiting with bats, shackles, and poles at the ready. Shaved heads, obscene tattoos, swastikas, leather jackets, torn white T-shirts, high boots, and fetid dispositions loudly evidenced their twisted, misguided, evil affiliations. Everyone on and in the bus correctly read the upcoming menacing signs and many screamed uncontrollably in dread.

The bus abruptly stopped a good fifty feet away from the facing mob and the quicker-witted bus passengers sitting below started to make their panic driven exits, trampling over each other in their haste.

At this point the skinheads attacked! They started with a barrage. First they hurled trashcans and rocks that crashed into the bus and sent shredded sharp tearing glass flying amongst the harried passengers to much damaging effect.

Heda's guards responded with a well-aimed cruncher salvo straight into the mob; knocking quite a few of them about forcefully back onto their asses amid the loud "whump, whump," retorts of their weapons.

Dave unhappily figured the mob to number at least a hundred or so of highly agitated thugs.

Their precarious position on top of the bus at once being duly noted by all, they turned and moved back toward the down steps when it happened.

The bus driver, an oft such harassed Senegalese, had had enough and seeing the happy product of the crunchers work, namely an opening hole in the confronting mob, nervously pushed forward on the joystick. Amid tumbling and flying exiting passengers and incoming dangerous flying objects this accelerated the bus suddenly and drove straight for the mob, his singular purpose to plow through them. The bus abruptly lurched ahead and careened and tumbled the passengers about especially those on top. The bus then accelerated faster and hit the mob hard with a loud thud and knocked many of them aside and amid many wounded screams from the skinheads it broke through them and headed up the street at full speed, headed for freedom.

The mob; many injured, were now even more angered, and weren't finished though, and brought out their heavy artillery. The air was soon filled with Molotov cocktails which slammed into the fleeing bus with some effectiveness. All at once the remaining frightened bus passengers found themselves more frightened by being stuck inside and traveling erratically up the street in a fiery bus.

One of the flaming cocktails hit the front of the bus and spewed fire in at the driver, causing him to flee his wheel and seat which caused the bus to swerve into a tall light pole. The bus crashed hard into the pole, knocking it down onto the top of the bus, and, the abrupt stop threw the remaining passengers roughly all about again.

The falling massive light narrowly missed killing Dave, Heda, Bruno, and the guards head on. It did hit one of the guards on the leg and he appeared to be limping badly but still ambulatory, Dave noticed as they all scurried as best they could toward the bus's front for some safety.

They weren't out of the woods yet though; the fire engulfing the rear of the bus was now spreading fast forward. Fire moved hotly toward them and soon surrounded them from the back up to the stairway. Heat swelled up from the first floor and caused the floor under Dave to heat up and begin to melt. His shoe soles stuck tackily as he sought to escape a burning death. They all pushed toward the front of the bus away from the flames, and Dave and Bruno momentarily shared a well practiced look of: "in the shit again."

All the while Heda was frantically yelling into her mike asking for much needed backup.

Dave figured that unless her backup were flying superheroes; their gooses were cooked in more ways than one. Besides, Dave now noticed that since encountering the mob that three flying drone buzzers had been shadowing the mob all along. Big Brother was watching and perhaps this tragedy was playing out according to his master plan.

The seething mob, its courage renewed by the burning red pyre before them, now advanced, screaming wildly, madly brandishing their lethal weapons, toward their hapless prey trapped in the stopped fiery bus.

~~~~~

The rubber sheet, as usual, didn't amply cover the blood pooled on the street, Albion noted. This part of the job he truly hated the most; the dirty part.

Pushing the sheet away gingerly he noted that singularity which his on scene officer; Harry Dickett had discretely noted; a missing left ear. The dead man appeared to be in his late thirties or early forties, white, round coarse features, and going to paunch due to excessive beer consumption. He had been sliced and mutilated; rather crudely it appeared, across his abdomen and throat, Albion noted.

The M.E. stated that the man had been killed here last night around midnight and dumped, not well hidden at all, to be discovered by this morning's working foot traffic.

Advancing age and thirty five years of this dirty work had eroded Frederick Egon Albion's much needed professional callousness to the point that he now for the first time happily looked forward to the escape of retirement. He knew in that instant he couldn't cut it anymore and felt shocked and relieved to openly face up to that cold hard fact at last. His mother, hoping for much better things for him; solicitor or doctor, or member of Parliament, had saddled him with a really bourgeoisie name. All it had ever done though for him was make him the target of his pugnacious peers growing up.

A wave of nausea suddenly washed over him and he retreated back a ways out of the cramped alleyway in order to catch his breath. Gaining the street he leaned back against a wall and rested. Pulling off his gloves, Albion frantically gasped for fresh air.

Desperately he sucked in the cool late morning sweet nectar into his cramped, constrained lungs in long, deep sips like a parched man until he was sated. His heart beat unnaturally hard and fast inside his bursting chest as he vainly sought his nitroglycerine tablets lost somewhere deep in his overcoat's pockets.

Dickett, as usual, noted Albion's discomfort and, making sure no one saw, offered him a swig from his silver flask. This time around, Albion happily took it and swallowed hard.

"Never get used to it, that is if you're normal," Dickett opined dryly.

"Right, right you are. Cheers," Albion chimed, breathing easier as the whiskey went down hot and soothing. Presently he breathed better, now feeling the world slowly ceasing to spin too fast under his shaky feet for him to once again maintain his normal equilibrium.

Pointing to the crimson blood trail out on the street leading up to the alley, Dickett remarked dryly, "He was initially attacked there and dragged into the alley where the perp worked him over quite a bit."

"Any witnesses?" Albion asked, now breathing shallowly.

"Not a one yet," Dickett answered dryly.

"Any I.D. on the victim?" Albion asked, wiping his sweaty brow.

"His wallet says he's one Elbert Stoner. He worked across town around the docks as a stevedore and minor union official. We're working on the time-line that led him here to his untimely end," Dickett reported, sneaking in a swig of his own.

"Good, I got to go," Albion said, still sweating nervously.

"I'll clean up here Inspector. The report will be on your desk early tomorrow," Dickett promised while gingerly patting Albion's broad back.

Relieved, but a bit embarrassed, Albion wanly smiled at his long-suffering brown skinned comrade and nodded while climbing into the back of his also rapidly aging 2011 Jaguar sedan.

As the dark, slouched, hulking form of his one true friend rapidly receded into the distance Albion heard over the police monitor: "Civil disturbance on Goodge, mob violence, bus on fire....all units respond!"

"Let's go take a look Alwynne," Albion ordered to his much harried driver.

~~~~~

The hot flames licked at their heels as they ran forward toward the front of the bus. Their only escape now appeared to be over the front and down onto the bus's cab to the ground.

The once menacing pole now served them well; as a shimmy pole escape down to the street. First one down safely was the uninjured guard, followed close by Dave and Heda. As he reached back up to help her she really saw him for the first time.

Noticing his trim physique, close cropped wavy black hair and young, strong handsome cocoa tinted face didn't do it for her. His light brown eyes looking up at her shining with genuine concern did though. For the first time in a long, long time her breath caught and her heart raced because of a man. She eagerly took his offered hand and gingerly jumped down right into his waiting arms. As she fell onto him and pressed her breasts hard into his chest Dave was dumbstruck at once by just how enticing and lovely a creature she was.

Bruno carried the injured guard down on his back and as they all found themselves cornered on the street hugging hard cement backed flat against a wall, with the burning bus between them and the approaching mob their hopes sunk anew. The loud mob began throwing their deadly Molotov cocktails at them again. One hit the wall close near them and burst into flame.

The BBC guards, to their credit, weren't about to go down without a fight. They aimed their weapons at the several incoming cocktails and discharging their weapons in unison, expertly hit most of them in mid air; pushing them right back from whence they came. The missiles bounced back into the approaching mob and savagely exploded amongst them and set quite a few surprised skinheads on fire. Now the skinheads had to dodge their own flaming, screaming, brothers rushing about here and there and Dave happily noticed that this broke up their attack momentarily.

Suddenly the bus's fuel cell exploded with a loud blast; hurling all nearby down to the ground amid an outwardly expanding wall of flying hot shrapnel and super heated hydrogen.

The skinheads slowly recovered from the fiery blast first and now fell on their hapless targets huddled and shell-shocked against the wall. They attacked in close with chain links and metal poles and swung hard for heads. One skinhead hit Dave upside his head with a chain which spun him around and back into the wall hard. Dave turned fast and remembering his time fighting in Iran and Syria during the U.S.'s second incursion; reacted from habit. Dave grabbed the end of the swinging chain and forcefully yanked the scruffy fellow hard, face first, into the wall where Dave proceeded to wrap the chain around his own fist and used the chain back on the man; pummeling him viciously about the head and shoulders. The bloody man then fell hard in a heap on the street, gurgling in his throat and bleeding heavily.

Bruno and the uninjured guard were happily busting heads and throwing skinheads into the fiery remains of the bus as Heda used her laser pistol to good advantage here and there on a succession of unfortunate skinheads who felt beating women was good etiquette. The injured guard leaned back against the wall and fired as best he could into the now fast dwindling but still crazed and determined mob.

Dave was rushed by two of them and he smashed one hard in the mouth sending his bloody teeth flying as the other; a particularly pale, odiously tattooed, skinny specimen raised his pole intending to brain Dave.

The man didn't get a chance to complete his swing though as his head suddenly connected hard with a baseball bat. The loud, seemingly hollow, sickening, crack that ensued caused all to pause momentarily and regard something new.

Wielding the old fashioned wooden American bat was a tall, grizzled, brown leather skinned derelict. With a scruffy, well-worn, torn tan overcoat and long graying nappy braided hair flying wildly he laid into the surprised skinheads with a vengeance and skill that was truly frightening to them. With nary a word, he batted them hard and often and swung with a strength and frenzy that seemed inhuman to all watching.

Dave thought him to be a mad homeless person from his soiled, gray tattered bum's outfit, but was glad to see him. The man's zeal caused the mob to pause, break, and fall back momentarily.

"You' all want to live? Follow me!" the scruffy man shouted as he suddenly stopped his frenzied attack and quickly headed back from whence he had come; a dark alley wedged between two buildings right up the street.

Not wanting to argue and seeing that their present position exposed on the street was untenable due to more incoming fiery cocktails, the hapless, scarred, blooded, victims wisely followed the odd man up the street and into the alley. All that is, except the wounded guard who couldn't keep up. At the alley's entrance he stopped and panted, "I'll cover for you all. I can't go on."

Fear and reason now warred in the minds of Heda and the other guard. She was adamantly against leaving her comrade here alone and Dave was loathe to leave her here despite her cold demeanor. Dave also didn't want to be forced to make another bad stand here in a really confined space in the face of the skinheads' superior force, but knew from experience that they all couldn't tarry there long and hope to live. The scruffy man continued on down the alley and yelled back for them to hurry.

"Roy, we can't leave you!" Heda sorrowfully implored the man as he suddenly sunk hard to the ground with blood streaming fast from his knee.

More cocktails landed and burst close by and fire now licked hotly at them again at the alley's entrance-.

"You know the drill. Get going!" Roy shouted bravely as he began firing anew into the fast approaching mob.

"We gotta go!" sadly urged the other guard, roughly grabbing Heda and pulling her down into the dark, dank, alley falling in behind the others.

Heda could hear the loud "whumps" of Roy's cruncher as they ran hard to catch up with the scruffy man fleeing ahead. The escapees ran down the dark alley and to a big rusty metal door which the scruffy man closed and bolted behind them. Before the door closed Dave had occasion to look back once and all he saw was a wall of fire growing at the end of the opposite end of the alleyway from where they had escaped.

The woeful sounds of Roy's cruncher soon faded into nothingness as they passed one door after another, all roughly but expertly bolted by the scruffy man. Their scruffy savior now lit a torch and holding it high over their heads led the way down, always down, this way and that down damp catwalks, long forgotten tunnels, and culverts, into a dark, unknown world that until today none of them ever imagined existed.

They soon passed into and under the wet smelly sewers and then the underground train rumbled hollowly far overhead and still they went down, down deeper under the dark smelly bowels of London; to where they didn't know.

Warren Freeman

Chapter 3

Saturday, October 1, 2016

"**W**hat in the bloody hell happened here?" Albion coughed angrily. His throat and nostrils smarted painfully from the fire and explosion caused acridity still floating heavily in the air. He sadly and nervously surveyed what recently used to be a quiet, peaceful, London street, early today in fact, not once upon a time.

The scene before him reminded him more of Tehran after the second 2007 invasion than present day London. The burned out bus and bodies being removed lent credence to the ferocity of whatever war that must have occurred here earlier. His on site detective; Sergeant Craig Oliver walked over to him, sweating bullets.

"The fight started farther down on Goodge, near as we can reckon. Skinheads numbering near a hundred attacked the bus there which ran from them until it hit that pole. Two charred bodies were taken out of the bus. Seven skins were found here dead outright. And from the burn marks on the street we reckon there'll be more. Twenty seven of the skins have showed up at hospital already, twelve with third degree burns," Oliver stated, pointing adroitly and barely hiding his glee.

"And---?" Albion asked haltingly.

"The BBC crew and the two Americans are missing except for one: Roy Tristan, BBC guard," Oliver said pointing to the passing body-bagged soul being carted away by police medical robotic personnel.

"We found him beaten to death over near that alley sans his cruncher," Oliver continued, pointing again.

"Notify the BBC to deactivate it and track it!" Albion barked.

"I'd rather have them detonate it!" Oliver said seriously, his blue eyes sparkling up.

"Cheeky, but no, it's too risky. The skinheads have possessed it for at least an hour. Their sick minds would surely make its exploding backfire on us," Albion soundly reasoned.

Albion then cast a mean glance upwards at the seven or so watcher drones zooming about above and asked, "What's their story?"

"Information Central says they were all out...in the entire district due to unusual solar flare activity!" Oliver answered, rolling his newly cloned sky blue eyes up around in his head sarcastically.

"Anybody canvass the alley?" Albion asked.

"Yes, and it's a clean empty dead end...! And it's got a big bolted door at the end. Rather queer it is. We're consulting city planning to determine where it goes," Oliver responded.

"Why---?" Albion asked knowingly.

Oliver knew exactly what the old man meant. Working together for over twenty five years had forged a useful mental bond between them.

"Don't know! The skinheads we collared have clammed up to a man. But it stinks. How these scruffy slackers remained that motivated while getting their asses kicked and burned just doesn't make sense. I imagine the targeting of the bus and the skin's zeal, and the drones' fortuitous absence will prominently turn up in your ledger," Oliver queried with a wry smile.

"Right you are Craig; right under highly unlikely and super, super suspicious," Albion remarked snidely, his nostrils stinging anew.

"You know, five minutes with that Extraminator thing and this case will be solved," Oliver spoke straight out in his naturally annoying way of getting right to the truth.

Albion nodded, the disturbing thought of going before the Ministry of Information's Home Council Secretary hat in hand again, balls on a plate, coming most painfully to mind.

A series of murders early last year in London had necessitated Albion's appearing before them asking for permission for an Extraminator sweep. Oddly they acquiesced immediately, saying that they were just about to call him to get his thoughts on whether they should use the device due to public safety concerns. Someone had killed by strangulation five housewives in their homes without nary a clue or a viable suspect. Public hue and cry had reached record highs.

The Extraminator sweep revealed the entirety of the crimes in all their gory details on disc. Albion diligently watched them all forwards and backwards until he swooned from fatigue.

All along they'd suspected a man or men, but the Extraminator showed a woman and a young boy, her nephew, gaining access to each house under pretense of gaining a charity contribution and once in attacking the helpless, unsuspecting women and then robbing them. The arrests had to be made with caution and be very circumspect because the police couldn't let it out that the Extraminator had solved the case as the Parliament and the Royals had banned the device's use in Britain for their own devious reasons.

"Sooner or later," Oliver said dryly.

"Yeah," Albion concurred. Sooner or later public opinion would bring things to a head with the government types feeling the lash, but Albion much preferred that this time they came to him. Also it didn't miss his notice that their continued silence on this particular matter was even more loudly deafening and getting louder day by day.

~~~~~

Clive Victor Waddell was enjoying his work today. "Oh yeah, I'm really, really, enjoying it," he mused, as he kicked Vince Sewell in his guts, again, hard.

"All you and your gang had to do was jack up one guy!" Clive spat evilly as he kicked the prone man again, this time in his swelling temple.

Vince moaned and rolled over, away from Clive, hoping to escape the avenging wrath and pain visiting him this day. He still smarted badly from the day's earlier fiasco. His cut, bruised, pained, and burned body vainly cried out to him for some relief soon.

"Five thousand £ pounds and I got nothing! Nothing!" cursed Clive delivering another fast savage kick to his victim's groin.

Blood spewed darkly out of the mouth of the prone man and Clive figured, from experience, that it was time to let up. The chance of getting Vince's blood on his brand spanking new grey sharkskin suit also figured heavily in Clive's unnaturally merciful decision.

Clive regarded the huddled, prone creature with utter contempt. The sorry man had haphazardly covered his entire thin, pale body with so many ugly red and blue tattoos that Clive barely recognized him as another white man. The fellow must subconsciously hate his own race so much to hide it so effectively under such bad taste scribbling passing for art, Clive mused with growing disgust.

"Clean yourself up and gather as many of your girlies together as you can. You still owe me something for my money," Clive barked and spat on the sickly-moaning man lying before him.

"I'll call you tonight with your orders. Be ready!" Clive growled as he brusquely turned to leave the depressingly dimly lit abandoned warehouse for the afternoon's sunny vista outside and beyond.

Vince, moaning sadly, gingerly rolled over onto his back and hugged his bruised ribs with his achingly thin arms while once again cursing his insatiable need for dope that now led him to this unholy, unloved, deadly chapter in his pointless life.

Warily watching his departing tormentor, Vince slowly retrieved from his jeans pants' pocket his last heroin patch. Slapping the patch onto his neck he waited for the sure fast relief his aching body so desperately craved. Suddenly waves of pure pleasure slammed jaggedly into his brain and washed down all over his battered body and soon he breathed much better.

Stepping out into the mid-afternoon Sun's warm glow rejuvenated Clive immensely. He stretched his arms behind him and preened a bit as he drank in the clean country air behind the safe house barn here in Croyden. The gaudy, overly expensive, long black fossil fueled Maybach four-door sedan waited patiently in the grassy hill above and Clive then slid into the back with all the catlike grace of the martial arts trained killer that he was. Inside, in the dark shadows, hidden from view, sat the tall quiet man; still as death.

"Here's your dosh and your next instructions. I want this one taken care of in the exact manner noted! This one my man Vince Sewell tailed, and shagged her, I hear, for a good week so she'll be the easiest so far. At least one part of this plan is working as planned," Clive said handing over a thick, money filled envelope to the man securely ensconced deep in the protecting shadows.

A long, coarse, hairy, gray-haired, pale white gnarled hand emerged from out of the dark and with an unearthly quickness, surely grasped the pay envelope with a strength and blazing speed that bothered Clive deep down in his cold, hard soul far more than he liked to admit.

~~~~~

The scruffy man led them at last to his final intended destination: a large well-lit circular chamber underground; exactly where they were they didn't know.

Their trip down the tunnels had been harrowing to say the least. Smelly dark sewers, swarms of rats, frightening noises in the dark; all now served to unnerve the escapees.

Locking the door, the derelict busied himself with providing warm beers, chips, and bandages all round.

The scruffy fellow wordlessly directed them all to take seating around the edges of the circular room on old ratty sofas. The fellows occupied one large threadbare item as Heda uneasily settled into a dusty chair. The room, a true cylinder, had once obviously had been a large holding tank of some type in a past life now easily contained all one would need to comfortably live for a while. A stove, refrigerator, air purifier, and sparse furniture, were all haphazardly arranged around the derelict's "home".

Dave could hear the loud sounds of falling water hitting the roof and sides of the cylinder and it gave him an eerie feeling of unease. He felt very claustrophobic, as though he was trapped inside a giant bell, with someone banging on the outside, probably day in and day out. No wonder the derelict acted so oddly, Dave soundly reasoned.

The derelict then proceeded to turn on a large screen Holo-TV situated on the far wall.

All except Heda took the beers happily but all sniffed the chips before gingerly, hesitantly, judiciously partaking.

"I don't get a lot of visitors, as you can probably tell. The restroom is over there," directed the derelict pointing to the only other door visible besides the one they had came in.

All politely declined, wisely, they were sure.

"Nice place you got here, but how do you survive way down here?" Dave rudely asked, unsuccessfully trying to cut the ice.

"I troll sonny. You'd be surprised how much valuable stuff comes floating my way," laughed the derelict.

"The valuables I sell on the surface and the bodies, well I sell them to the morgues and hospitals," he continued smiling evilly.

A long pregnant pause followed from the new visitors.

"I'm Heda Marish, BBC. This is Jeffrey Mills my guard and those two are Dave Asher and Bruno Guntz. They're from America. We're awfully thankful to you, Allah be praised," Heda said, pointing out her compatriots, and shockingly, to Dave, exhibiting the first occasion of polite manners he'd actually witnessed in England in three days.

"Don't mention it missy," replied the derelict, nervously switching his eyes oddly to and fro. "It was my mistake."

"Your mistake---? Come again," Bruno asked as he applied a bandage to his cut, bruised right hand.

"I thought you had that Extrarotasoda thing, though now I hear, in the spirit of new market capitalism, you call it the new and improved higher priced Extraminator. That's the only reason I busted up your fun and games with those Neo-

Nazis. I never interrupt you surface creatures while you're feeding on each other. It appears I was wrong, you don't have it," admitted the derelict sadly.

"The police took it. And, bottom dweller, who are you?" asked Dave angrily.

"I'm Alberto Arethusa Harvernera!" defiantly heralded back the derelict striking a very contrived pose with arms on hips, legs slung wide, and head cocked back in an exaggerated pose of utter bravado and defiance.

Laughter from the seated group greeted the derelict's latest odd act.

"Why did you want the Extraminator?" asked Heda, snickering.

Nonplused, Alberto went on with: "I wanted to see if something I found down here is what I think it was. You'll see it on the way up later."

"You're Harvernera? That's rich," said Dave laughing and slapping his thigh hard.

"I am he, and I can prove it," Alberto replied seriously.

"Harvernera hit it big in Hollywood six years ago then vanished. He made millions, millions. If you are him why are you here, in this stinking hole?" Dave asked snidely.

"I'm seeking truth, sonny. Hollywood set me up with this leading lady, see... They said she was the prettiest thing ever. When I saw her all I saw was her two ugly brothers looking right back at me, which didn't help my love scenes with her at all. Course she sported some fine boobs, but she still looked in the face like her really homely two male siblings. No matter how long they told me she was fine, I just couldn't see it. I wondered if something was wrong with me, but finally I figured out that the studio bosses, and my agent too, they were the one's who were brainwashed and I wasn't. That lie and others they told me led me to question," Alberto said swinging his head around again oddly.

"Question what?" Heda snappily asked now, with a start, recognizing that under that all that caked on grime and dirty nappy hair before her stood a disheveled shell of a man that was really "The Harvernera." Harvernera the great! Harvernera; the handsomest man in Hollywood and the greatest actor in ten years! Or so his press releases oft claimed.

She could actually see the personage of the once handsome heartthrob slowly emerge to her mind's eye from under years of purposeful neglect. She looked deep and saw that his bright brown eyes still twinkled with the legendary fire that had caused millions of panting women to flock to his movies, but she personally, always considered him at most a studio contrived personality not a genuine accomplished actor.

"Everything! I had to get out of there to think and get my soul back. I hate them, the bosses, they told me to look past the truth and see just what they wanted me to see and everything would be fine. I couldn't, I just couldn't; try as I did. Lord knows I tried!" Alberto replied, smiling wryly back at Heda with his big brown eyes tearing up.

Alberto then agilely climbed up the wall shelves and pulled out his old scrapbooks and threw them down on the dusty old table in front of the doubters.

"Take a good look kids, you won't have long," Alberto informed them abruptly.

"What?" they all asked in unpracticed unison.

"I'm putting you all out on the street tonight. All that mess topside will blow over soon. I can't afford the police looking down here too long," Alberto cried, his head twitching anew.

"Have you found what you sought?" Heda asked sympathetically.

"I'm a lot closer than I ever was," Alberto said scratching his left ear nervously.

"Did you hear that?" Alberto asked suddenly.

"What?" Heda asked, dumbfounded.

"A chirping sound, I hear it all the time in my left ear. Did you hear it?" Alberto asked, pleadingly.

Dave, Bruno, and Jeff rolled their eyes in unison.

Heda smiled sadly and patted Alberto's hand.

The old fashioned Holo-TV then projected a hologram down onto the area of the floor before the seated people showing in colorful 3-D life-sized visions the street far above including the burned out bus on the surface and the police diligently milling about.

The cute, blond, usually perky, news announcer was blandly mouthing a pre-written précis chronicling the day's horrific events on Goodge Street. Behind her were pasted pictures of those very same survivors now assembled around and viewing the images. Below her, the ticker tape said: "Moslem Jihadists advance on Cairo!.......GM retakes first place, first time in ten years on sale of electric autos!.....Food riot breaks out on moon base, six injured!.....Newly discovered earth sized planets number rises to 731!....Jerry Springer show reruns cancelled!"

Heda again vigorously tapped her headset and attempted to contact the BBC.

"That won't work down here honey, too much rock betwixt here and the surface," Alberto stated, smiling.

Heda sat back sadly.

"Why is all this happening? Am I the only one here that thinks all this crap that has been happening to us is rather strange?" Dave asked.

This question was met by quiet ignorance from all.

Dave impulsively walked in amongst and between the three dimensional images with disgust right over to Heda's sofa and asked, "Can anyone...? Heda, tell me what the hell is going on? Why are your countrymen trying to kill us? Or is all this mayhem standard operating procedure around here?"

Heda sat shaking her head disgustedly since she didn't have an answer.

"Us? Better question is, which one of you is it that they're after?" Alberto piped in ominously.

All looked about at each other suspiciously now with many new concerns arising.

~~~~~

"Same M.O.! I've been over the ancient records twice. It's uncanny how these cuts almost perfectly mirror the Ripper's first victim, Mary Ann Nichols, killed August 31, 1888. Same type of cut to the throat, same exposed vertebrae, and the same stomach wounds," said Dr. Harry Griscom, the shaggy, jovially rotund, brown haired much harried M.E. in his usual boring monotonous tone.

"You did say almost?" Albion queried, blanching.

"You're paying attention today," Griscom retorted snidely.

Albion retreated farther back flush against the wall and further back into his own world as the doctor warmed up to his subject.

"See here: Throat cut lengthwise, abdomen opened with long vertical slashing cuts," the be-speckled, balding, doctor continued affording the green faced Albion an all too good view of the cadaver to presently suit him.

Albion choked back the growing bile he invariably expected to feel coming up his esophagus whenever he found himself down here in the cold, morose, morgue.

"Thanks, but I'll take your word," Albion wheezed, retreating back from the doctor and his latest specimen; Elbert Stoner.

"Don't be a sissy, man," Dr. Griscom chided opening the prone cadaver's chest for more of his well practiced probing.

Albion now desperately clutched his chest, over his heart, and turned quite pale in the face.

"Egon, why don't you get that thing replaced? I reckon that Doctor Everett has a perfectly good substitute waiting for you at the organ bank," Griscom said without missing a probing motion.

"Chester," Albion barked back, angrily mimicking Griscom's unauthorized use of his middle name in jest. "I'll do it when I'm good and ready." Albion spoke this knowingly. He knew for an unhappy fact that Griscom and Everett were golf buddies and shared way too much patient information between them.

"One thing; this fellow's a liter light in the blood department," Griscom remarked, "any ideas about why?"

Albion shook his head in the negative even as his mind raced, all too certain now where Jack got his ink now.

"Anything else unusual---?" Albion queried, fishing.

"How so?" replied the doctor feigning naivety.

"You know, anything that might lead you to conclude that there's some supernatural activity afoot?" Albion asked nervously, quite embarrassed by the question.

Griscom laughed and then regarded the detective gravely with some obvious professional concern.

"Not at all. Nothing new here, that is nothing that I haven't seen before. Nothing here says your "Jack" is a ghost or demon and not a man," Griscom said suppressing another laugh.

Nothing?" Albion asked again, sheepishly.

The doctor just shook his head in disgust.

As Albion left he heard the doctor shout behind him: "Don't be a sissy, man. Don't wait for your ticker to fail you. Haste favors the living!"

It was a bit later that Dr. Griscom remembered the report that he'd forgotten to give Albion from the little information that the Ministry leaked to New Scotland Yard's forensics department upstairs regarding their analysis of the confiscated Extraminator's disk. It had shown a face that after they analyzed it, they tentatively made an identification of the 1888 Ripper.

Unfortunately when he remembered and ran after Albion, Albion was nowhere to be seen.

~~~~~

Their hospital visit over, Dave met his surly associates in the lobby.

Alberto easily led them up to the surface as he had promised, depositing them safely on a well traveled street, before taking his leave.

He had stopped only once on the way up to show them what had led him to rescue them. It turned out to be a partially buried creature's bleached bones sticking out of the tunnel wall. All now marveled at the beast's size which they reckoned to be somewhere around a hundred feet long. Its long sharp teeth lent credence to its chief activity while living and all were glad not to have met up with him when he was alive.

Lying on the hospital bed after swiping his medical card, Dave was being serviced by the company doctors in America by remote procedure. This was necessary because the English routinely refused medical care and financial liability for foreigners.

The all too, for his profession, young looking American doctor, using Wi-Fi uplink, utilized the English hospital's equipment to mend Dave. The hospital's medical machines sat in an arc above him and repaired, dressed, and poured medical glue into his lacerations and wounds all the while directed by a doctor way across the Atlantic. It was odd to Dave to lie there as the machine quietly worked on him with its cold metallic tentacles, as he watched the wall mounted video-screen. The silver screen produced the face of the American doctor who, while directing the medical machine, talked to him soothingly as though nothing was out of the ordinary.

Watching an obviously malfunctioning hospital service robot bang into a wall over and over, Dave was happy to have his uplink doctor working on him and he wondered how Bruno was enjoying his similar experience.

Regarding their sullen faces, after his medical session, Dave knew Heda had finally reported in and bad things were ahead. Best to cut it off in the bud, he reasoned.

"I'm famished, and I'm getting me a meal and a beer and a whiskey! Got that? And before anyone raises any objections, I don't give a damn what you all do!" Dave said resolutely as he pushed his way out the hospital doors and headed up the street.

Heda began to tell him that Albion wanted them to wait for him there at hospital but Dave's receding back convinced her that is was better to defer this time.

They all followed without a protest. He found a restaurant two blocks north and soon all were eating, drinking, and enjoying the restaurant's house band with gusto.

Later, taking his leave from the table, Dave hit the restroom. Inside after his much needed urinal stop he stood at the far basin washing his hands when he looked up in the glass and noticed them flanking him. How he'd missed them Dave couldn't figure; they must have moved silently as cats to sneak up on him like this. There were three of them and all were way bigger, browner, and balder than Bruno, and they were close behind him, real close.

"Take it easy sport, and this won't take long," one big man warned grabbing Dave and spinning him around.

"What?" Dave answered, vainly attempting to free himself from the big man's giant ham hock of a hand.

The large, brown, robust fellow laughed and pushed Dave hard against the wall where another big goon joined him in holding Dave against the wall, the third stood by the door with a Colt pistol in his hand.

"Scan him!" barked a fellow that Dave hadn't noticed before, in a deep, rich baritone voice.

This one was a good foot shorter, but more distinguished, and just as brown and bald as the others though he wore a manicured goatee and mustache, and was dressed much richer in genuine black leather and suede. Dave took him to be the boss.

Goon number one scanned Dave with a small device that shot out an odd green glow which covered Dave from head to toe. At once the device glowed red and goon number one placed it up against Dave's lapel. The device then hummed softly and turned a soft blue.

Dave was highly surprised and wondered what had been stuck to him and for how long had it been there.

"What's that?" Dave asked.

"Got it," goon number one laughed ignoring Dave's question as he passed the bluish glowing device back to his boss.

The boss took the thing and held it real close to his heart and breathing in heavily, smiled the smile of the truly happy. Placing the device in his inside jacket pocket the man then regarded Dave, his flashing, dark green eyes piercing, with some unknown but serious interest.

"Do you know who I am?" the "boss man" asked regally.

"No," Dave answered, struggling again against the two goons still holding him tight.

"That's expected, since you don't even know who you are," the man stated evenly.

"What?" Dave asked, puzzled.

"I'm Benjamin J. Cresasern, the most hated black man in the whole wide world. Surely you've heard of me? I own the company that markets the Light Discernment Extraminator."

"Nice to meet you fella. I'm Dave Asher, catcher extraordinaire," Dave jested back flippantly.

"You think you're Dave Asher but that isn't so. The orphanage made up that name for you; that is after they found you abandoned on a Rittenhouse Square Park bench in Philadelphia one cold night in mid 1989 in a basket," Cresasern said smugly, motioning to have Dave released.

Dave; verbally slapped in the face and upset at the man's troubling and painfully sharp surprising revelation, nevertheless now breathed a lot easier without the two big men leaning on his chest.

"Park bench? Basket---?" Dave echoed, shakily.

"Sorry, but as a catcher surely you of all people should be able to handle the truth, especially when it pertains to you," Cresasern argued coldly, evenly.

"I've heard of you. What was that that you took from my jacket lapel?" Dave asked again, inwardly shaking with anger and confusion and wondering how truthful what the man had just said was.

"None of your damn business!" barked goon number one, slapping Dave hard back into the wall with a large backhand blow.

"That's enough of that!" shouted Cresasern, admonishing his guard sternly.

"Black Science isn't about savagery," he continued softer, "we're about helping mankind!"

"Black Science?" Dave echoed, quite surprised at hearing that term from a black man.

"What have you got to do with Black Science?" Dave queried.

"In the beginning we invented it, the science part that is. Our enemies gave it the name Black Science for their own purposes of misinformation. I and Walter Grimmet invented certain devices and instead of having them stolen by the big holding companies, as was usual, we kept and produced our inventions and the profits I might add. Walter invented the L.E.D. and I invented the Clowder receptacle that converts the Tesla Spire's air-borne energy to everyone's everyday use all around the world," Cresasern crowed proudly.

"Now the world's capitalists' motto is not to beat us but to join us, though many won't admit it Black Science is now really Human Science. Our enemies keep the "Black" in play to keep the non-brown hued populaces of the world riled up against fair competition," Cresasern continued.

"We now have a pollution free electric auto engine capable of 250 horsepower, a filtration system for industrial plants that remover 90% of all wastes, and of course the Tesla Spire; an energy source that circumvents the moneyed good old boy's big oil energy monopoly. We've also cut world-wide pollution significantly and thus started the reversal of global warming, which "they" said couldn't be done so fast. We got tired of the good old boy; world-wide monopolistic energy production capitalist ruining the planet and gouging the consumer with an inefficient energy source that had outlived its usefulness. Thus we took over and stole his breakfast, lunch, and soon we'll have his dinner. We took the steering wheel away from the man driving and now we're piloting this car. He was rich and powerful to be sure but also quite drunk and didn't know where he was going anyway," Cresasern preached, smiling broadly.

Bruno entered the bathroom and immediately found a cold pistol barrel jammed hard up against his head.

"Stand still over there Bruno, and everything will be alright real soon, our business is almost over here," Cresasern ordered sternly.

Bruno complied silently.

"How were you able to do what you did?" Dave asked, truly amazed at what they had accomplished.

"We realized firstly that we were up against not just the world's corrupt capitalist power structure but principalities, so we beseeched GOD to help us. Thankfully GOD helped us. Our next big step, and our most dangerous I may add, is to stop all war and then disease in Africa by running the demons, real and human, out of the continent. Once that's done; the indigenous people there will enjoy the peace and unlimited business opportunities of permanent continental unity, and prosperity. No longer will they be stuck to the arms dealers for their main commerce. Africa will bloom and become a world class power money house, as it should be. And for that we must thank you Dave," Cresasern gushed, happily hugging Dave in a brotherly fashion.

"What?" Dave asked, dumbfounded.

Without another word Cresasern smugly patted his jacket containing the device and knowingly smiled at Dave and as if on cue, the four men abruptly left Dave and Bruno alone in the restroom pondering what had just happened.

"Let's keep this quiet to our new friends, we'll discuss it together later," Dave advised wisely.

Dave and Bruno returned to their table. their compatriots none the wiser to the events in the restroom, and soon all decided to call it a night. They all went back to the Carlton Arms for a peaceful night sleep.

~~~~~

Dickett leaned against the cold, hard, slate Gothic styled cloistered wall and felt small. Small, real small, he thought.

Kicking and screaming, literally, in protest Albion had dragged him over here deep into the hallowed bowels of King's College on Strand. He felt very small among the tall walls, gargoyles, and big brains happily toiling here as he watched the two old friends, colleagues, and more often; opponents, spar before him. Albion towered over his friend, the small, wiry, bushy dirty blond haired, Professor Billingsly as he harangued the smaller man for an answer.

"Why me?" Professor Billingsly asked. "Your police scientists couldn't help you?"

"Can I get a straight answer Bill?" Albion asked, quite exasperated now.

Billingsly puffed on his ivory meerschaum with that false look of studied intelligence that he had cultivated for over twenty five years with much personal and professional success. His thick brown hair shook and he pondered seriously as he posed as if on the edge of a precipice.

"There are mainly two types of physicists; those that believe in the earth, this universe, and myriad clustered dimensions, with no GOD, no heaven, no hell, all motivated by the laws of physics and nature, whatever they are, and the other type, of which I belong. We believe in all that the former group does with the addition that we believe, and believe, that's the key word, in GOD, heaven, and hell. We believe that GOD made and animates it all even now for his own unknown purposes which we humans probably will never fathom," Billingsly said puffing again the sweet pungent Indian blend he so loved.

Albion threw his hands up in despair and cried, "Your point?"

"The Extraminator doesn't give off enough energy to disrupt the space-time-continuum in the least. It simply sifts through past light waves and reconstructs a picture with a seventy five percent infallible rating of the past. The other twenty five percent it fills in with a logarithm program that is ninety seven percent accurate. As a scientist I tell you that that device cannot pull anything out of the past in a real three dimensional level of existence. The entire human race, for as long as we've existed, hasn't yet created enough energy to time travel. As a scientist I assure you of this!" Billingsly said haughtily.

"As a scientist---?" Albion asked nervously.

"As a man who believes in things he doesn't really understand I must say that I don't know what GOD or demons can do," Billingsly explained seriously.

Albion simply shook his head, and asked, "Can you be more specific?"

"There is absolutely no scientifically observable or measurable proof that I'm aware of; that GOD, heaven, hell, or demons exist, or don't exist for that matter! If you were to somehow scientifically record a demon, well then, the measurable proof of one of the four things I just mentioned would lend scientific credence to the other three! In effect you would shake man's total world view and knowledge up so much that it would seriously reverberate forever throughout the scientific and religious communities! Billingsly gushed.

"Really?" Albion asked, "Why?"

"Faith, no matter how strong it is in us; the difference between our believing in something with absolutely no proof and the knowing of something to be a scientifically provable fact, well, the difference between those two concepts can be measured in light years! The "knowing" rather than blind faith in something would radically change human existence on this planet forever! The wild card is that which we don't know anything about," Billingsly stated, quite sadly it appeared to Dickett.

Dickett now became quite interested in the argument and listened in more closely, totally forgetting his cold perch against the wall.

"Can it be a demon? Can the reason Jack The Ripper wasn't identified or caught in 1888 be that he, it, actually escaped from that time over into this time? Can that evil time travel?" Albion shouted as his frustration grew.

"Of course it can be. Anything can be. We just don't know enough about the unknown to explain away everything in history. I can tell you this, good and evil have existed together since GOD created them each, down through the ages, both somehow surviving all that time threw at them," he continued drolly, tapping down his pipe.

"No straight answer then?" Albion asked at last.

"I just ain't got it!" Billingsly admitted, finally.

~~~~~

Dave regarded his room number "517" with an almost spooky intuition. Something was wrong with that number, he knew, but as tired as he was he couldn't quite fathom the unseen, undecipherable puzzle right before him.

Meeting Benjamin Cresasern had been a truly enlightening experience, in more ways than one. The man had reawakened some old, long suppressed memories in him as well as reopening a wound he'd thought was healed long ago. With a rush the anger returned, the anger of growing up parentless, abandoned, without benefit of natural loving parents, all this now hurt him anew. His mentally seeing painful visions of himself as a child being left alone on a cold, hard, park bench only served to dull his attention on the present to his unseen but imminent detriment.

Dave swiped his room key card in the slot and entered looking forward to some peaceful sleep. He was sleepily reaching for the light switch with his left hand when he was roughly grabbed and yanked into the room and spun around. A sharp fist swiftly came out of the dark and hit him hard, square between his eyes propelling him back into the room onto the floor with a loud thud. Seeing stars and tasting his own blood, Dave fell hard against the floor as he fought to maintain consciousness. He was roughly picked up by strong hands and soon stood facing a painfully bright, blinding, white light shining straight into his face. Though he couldn't see well he speculated from the barely visible pointy spikes atop their heads, that the fellows holding him were skinheads.

"He's clean but he's been scanned recently," reported one of the men roughly holding Dave up.

"Damn it! Where is it?" snottily shouted a man from behind the bright, painfully blinding light, standing a ways back away from those holding Dave up on shaky legs.

I don't know what you're talking about," Dave lied, oddly finding that he was unable to support his own weight on his own feet.

A hard fist slammed roughly into Dave's stomach, painfully doubling him over.

"I don't like black wanker liars! And since you don't have what I want and won't talk straight with me I don't give a shite for your life!--- Chuck him!" screamed the overly agitated man in an oddly high pitched accent Dave resolved to remember well if he survived this night.

Suddenly Dave was savagely picked up by at least three fellows, he figured groggily. They proceeded to carry him high up on their shoulders as they ran swiftly toward the only window in the suite.

Dave got really scared then and yelled and threw one arm over his face as the men propelled him viciously right into the window with as much force as they could muster.

Dave hit the window really hard with a loud crash, head first, and shattered the glass and wooden panes as his body smashed hard straight through the window. Dave then unhappily found himself, along with many pieces of flying glass shards and splintered wood pieces, soaring without benefit of the support of an airplane fast out into the frighteningly cool London night air high up, way too high up!

Dave felt his guts tighten up with swiftly welling up fear running up into his chest and suddenly remembering his frightening childhood dreams of falling, he yelled a loud, plaintive, primal scream full of the fear of impending death.

As he sailed, soaring, free falling, he screamed loudly anew as his arms vainly flailed out in a breast stroke swimming motion; flailing against the all too thin dark night air, hopefully for the sake of somehow saving his now too quickly passing away life!

Chapter 4

Saturday, October 1, 2016

Heda slipped slowly into the warm, soothing, bubbling soapy water filled tub and felt all at once human again. She slowly, adoringly, sipped a cool mineral water while tuning in the illegal, to the lower class; or as the upper classes called them: S.B.P., standing for Smaller British People, American History channel.

The requested scene appeared on the rim of her tub in its usual three-dimensional clarity, albeit at one third normal size, this time showing the collision of an American Army Air Force prototype UFO and a real UFO over Roswell New Mexico in 1947.

Having seen this one many times before, she flipped channels to something more soothing, she hoped the Home Improvement Channel. Inadvertently she hit the news and was treated to the sight of fire and billowing smoke. The news caster, a particularly bland young man, went on boringly about the American, Syrian, and Russian embassies being firebombed by skinheads tonight. Next up was the latest fist fight between the British U.N. ambassador Neville Scottley and his French counterpart; Pierre Pompladou. The two dignitaries were caught swinging away at each other as the French newscaster commented, "The British are still embarrassed and angry that the events of August 30th, 1997 came out to show who was driving the chase cars that ran Princess Diana's Mercedes into the wall in the tunnel below Place de L'Alma."

Heda dozed a bit since none of this was new to her.

In her semi-sleep she turned east toward Mecca for her usual daily prayers and saw the large, deep brown, forlorn eyes and handsome face of Dave Asher looking back at her from afar. Knowing that she was dreaming she lazily went with it, though it troubled her somewhat that that fellow was in her dream. Dave proceeded to climb over a dream fence and join her and sat with her peacefully with a cheap Mexican beer in his hand.

The phone suddenly rang, waking her up.

For a split second his snide, evilly expressive, square jawed visage hovered, openly leering, right above her vulnerable nakedness in the tub, in frightening three-dimensional clarity, until she hit the privacy button that is.

"Hi honey. Miss me? I miss you. Can I swing by in a bit?" it cajoled.

Listening without a word, Heda heard the thick, sickly sweet voice that she had once waited for with bated breath. But now it only served to curdle her skin, it a begging with its usual lies.

"Piss off Clive!" Heda screamed as she slammed her fist down on the receiver button, hard.

"That sure felt good," she murmured to herself.

Leaning back in the warming tub she could hear her mother in Karachi once again saying, "Don't believe half of what the Moslem boys say Heda, and nothing the Christian boys said; they're all hypocrites at all times!"

Heda smiled, her mother had been half right. In her own experiences in the western world it had been proven that both Moslem and Christian men were hypocrites and liars in most all things, especially when it came to women. Heda had divorced herself from Islamic, Asian, and Pakistani men as potential mates when she was eight years old. That's when her father had run off with his Jihadist Asian male lover. Oddly, she now realized that she had, and was still taking her father's desertion far worse than her mother and younger sisters ever had.

Her mother then bravely continued her own quiet life without her husband as though his leaving was nothing important while Heda absolutely fumed almost daily over it. Not a day passed without her painfully reliving his leaving that dank, dreary, awful Saturday morning. The whys of her mother's passive reaction were best left undiscovered, she felt as time matured her; leaving her truly frightened about what she might discover.

Now, not having any lesbian tendencies in the least, unlike half her girlfriends, she was caught between the rock: the western Christian white man and the hard place: the western Christian black man; Heda felt trapped. Rebuffing Clive this night had been the most pleasurable activity she had experienced with him since they'd met a year ago and she soon slipped deeper into the warm bubbly water and soon slept the sleep of the truly happy.

~~~~~

Albion cursed his usual bad luck. Of all the London hospitals; they just had to pick Saint Alban's.

"I'll duck in and duck out with them quick as a jackrabbit," he hoped ruefully.

Of course, they weren't in the lobby as hoped. Albion reluctantly sauntered over to the information desk and inquired about his expected charges.

While conversing with the near-sighted, myopic, matronly nurse he learned that they had left some thirty minutes ago. Albion sadly scrutinized her stooped posture and grey hair barely framing her tired wrinkled face with his own tired eyes and wondered if her tired eyes saw the same old novel in him; a person caught in time, a victim of old age stuck forever? Had they both ever been young? From the looks of her she looked like she had been born old, and so did he, he reckoned musing, slipping down again into a dangerous hyperbole.

Suddenly he felt the familiar tap on his shoulder that he dreaded but knew awaited him. Turning, he saw the dreaded green eyed cold stare of Doctor Clarence Everett, his dreaded cardiologist and what's worst; his brother-in-law.

"Come with me," implored Everett, roughly grabbing Albion's right arm and pulling him into a near room.

"Take your coat and shirt off!" ordered the tall, robustly built doctor tersely.

Albion meekly complied and soon he felt the cold stethoscope rummaging rudely against his sparse, graying chest hairs.

Everett then regarded him seriously and said sadly, "I'll give you a month on the outside before I'll be seeing you cold and stiff and gushing full of formaldehyde prone in your casket!"

"That's it?" Albion asked meekly, the full import of his death sentence hitting him blankly with no measurable human feeling or expected reaction on his part. He realized that he just didn't care if he lived or died, though he didn't know why, and that, that really bothered him. Of course he always listened to Everett because he was the only one in Florence's family of ignorant, needy, overbearing, domineering idiots that exhibited even one bit of good sense.

"I'm scheduling you for Monday, noon, three days hence. I have a replacement heart cloned from your own cells on ice for you, and have had for the past four months. I'm done dawdling with you Egon. Get your affairs in order and you better tell Florence, today, or I will!" Everett angrily fumed as he exited, leaving Albion shirtless and alone in the room with his chilly chest and unfathomed haywire emotions and of course, his growing fears about the nothingness of his life.

~~~~~

Dave felt a little bit relieved, but not much.

There before him loomed the ledge of the building next door. Perhaps his forward momentum would carry him all the way across the alley to safety, he hoped. He now blessed the fact that the hotel management hadn't heeded his request for a room with more of a view than only the building next door's old brick alley way facade.

His hope and joy lasted only a second as he felt gravity pull and grab him and stop his forward impetus and replace it with the sickening feeling of the beginning of his vertical descent at an all too frightening increasing speed. Dave now sickeningly realized that he wouldn't reach the ledge or the building at all but would soon fall to his death in the dark alley below. As he fell downwards, he still hopelessly, instinctively, flailed about vainly with his arms.

Suddenly he grasped onto something and held on for all he was worth with both hands, thus breaking his fall.

In the dark as he hung precariously from his perch, Dave realized that he had grabbed onto a flying surveillance drone, but just barely. The silver, oval shaped buzzer shook violently trying to free itself of its unwanted baggage as Dave held on for dear life.

In the dim light Dave noticed several other drones close by as evidenced by their silvery outlines and he wondered, while happy for the unexpected help, what were they were doing hovering around a dark alleyway at this time of night. The drone now began to sputter and violently weave back and forth, then it exuded a sharp blast of static electricity along its entire epidermis shocking Dave and causing him to release his grip as he shredded a piece of its outside molding in his hand in a vain attempt to hold on.

Shucked from his unwilling "friend", Dave found himself once again without support and, discarding the useless molding, he began his downward spiral anew with his hands flailing outwards vainly once again.

Surprisingly, his flailing right hand then snagged onto something again, this time something greasy, hard, and thin! Without thinking, Dave closed his fist and held hard on to whatever it was, stopping his descent momentarily. Swinging to and fro, he now realized it was a cable stretching between the two buildings. He hoped it wasn't electrified as he struggled, by swinging up his other arm, to get a good grip. This caused his body's downward plummet to change direction back towards the even deeper blackness of the dead end alley as he fought to live.

However, the cable proved to be too greasy and his grip slipped away and he fell once again, this time toward the juncture of the buildings below. He fell down onto something then with a loud, bone crunching sound that scarily signaled to him a serious injury; that is if he lived, he laughed to himself.

Dave now took stock of his present condition and concluded that he had fell right onto the top of a curved light pole, a broken one at that as it didn't illuminate the encompassing darkness below at all.

Too weak to grasp onto the pole, he slipped down off the pole and fell backwards down into the darkness onto a pile of smelly trash bags piled up beside a dumpster. He hit hard and lay still for a bit wondering if he was dead or alive.

Dragging himself up gingerly, with aching muscles, from his smelly street bed Dave felt rather than saw it.

In the darkness he couldn't see much, in fact he saw nothing but shadows on shadows. Still he quickly grabbed a trash bag up and held it before him instinctively. The bag shredded instantly and spewed its fetid contents out onto the dark street before Dave. Without further thought Dave picked up a trash can lid and holding its handle tight, he swung it outward before him hard. His swing was met unexpectedly by a loud resounding "clang" and Dave knew he had hit something of a metallic nature, but what?

Dave now yelled, "Help---!"

To whom he was yelling he didn't know, but yelling seemed like a good idea at this time. It certainly made him feel a bit better. Keeping his lid as shield, he grabbed up another trash bag, and hurled it forward out into the darkness, where to he didn't know.

Dave peered ahead into the thick darkness and now he sensed, without actually seeing it; it! It was, as well as he could tell by the singular, sliver of a glint, he was sure, a long shiny knife and it was attached to a long arm of an odd, man-like creature that resembled nothing so much as a large dark pyramid.

Dave felt the first pangs of fear ripple slowly up his back. The pyramid creature curiously, silently, regarded Dave for a moment then backed away from him in an eerie gliding motion that Dave was almost sure wasn't a man's normal walk.

The sounds of a bobby's whistle approaching now rudely interrupted the dangerous drama in the dark alley.

As the murky creature backed away Dave saw the white and red fuzzy patch revealed lying on the street and he knew without seeing it clearly that he was seeing a body!

The dark creature backed away up on to the pavement and began to rapidly diminish. That's what it seemed like, as well as Dave could tell. As best as Dave could discern with his limited vision, the monster oozed, or poured itself, down into the pavement until it was no more.

Not believing what he was almost seeing Dave felt pure, cold, fear sneak up on him again. Suddenly, the hard, ragged, scraping sound of metal on concrete; a manhole cover he figured, helped Dave's confused mind make some rational sense of what was happening, but not much.

Dave slowly ventured forward and soon stood above the white and red and saw what he didn't really want to see.

The woman had once been quite beautiful, he was sure. Now she lay splayed out, wide-eyed, bloody, and butchered in a most perverse way. Dave turned his head away from her as the alley was instantly flooded with the eye burning glare of overbearing, blinding, white light.

"Don't move! Hands up!" shouted someone from behind the blinding lights.

Dave dumbly complied as many rough hands grabbed him and cuffed him.

As they led him out of the dark alley and into the police car he heard the cry echoing up and down the streets, gaining strength as it went on and on.

"They got him! They got him! They got the Ripper!"

~~~~~

Bruno heard a loud crash from directly above him upstairs and bolted from the bed half asleep. Something flew down past his window but he couldn't make it out since he was only half awake. Without thinking he sleepily left his room and ran for the fire escape, fear tugging at his mind. He knew Dave occupied the room directly above him and not aware of what was actually happening he sensed that this was just too much happening not to be something serious.

He hit the door with a loud bang and unexpectedly came face to face with a thin, tattooed, skinhead barreling down the steps. The two men collided at once and the smaller skinhead fell back on the floor with an angry curse that Bruno couldn't understand. And, recognizing the fellow from the bus burning, and not wishing to know what the skinhead was cursing about, Bruno simply punched him hard in the head as he rose, causing the man to fall back hard against the wall and then tumbling forward down the steps amid many loud crunching sounds.

Without giving the fellow another glance, Bruno continued up the stairs and soon found himself outside Dave's room with its door ajar.

The elevator door down the hall closed with a chime and glancing that way, Bruno saw only the legs of a grey sharkskin suit entering the elevator.

Entering Dave's empty room Bruno immediately saw that the window was smashed and he ran to it. Gazing down into the darkness of the street below he saw shadows tussling, it looked like. Suddenly he heard in the darkness below the sharp clang of metal on metal and then Dave calling, "Help---!"

Bruno now ran from the room and toward the downward stairs where, on the stairwell below he encountered the skinhead once again. The fellow was moaning and rising up and Bruno purposefully kicked him hard in the head as he jumped over him on his downward flight. The fellow yelled in pain and sprawled fast down the stairs again in a bone crunching tumble behind Bruno.

Gaining the street and the alley around back of the hotel Bruno arrived panting, just in time to see the police take Dave away in cuffs.

Glancing back up to the fifth story window where Dave must have came tumbling down from Bruno experienced a sense of "déjà vu" with a jolting start and a cold sweat.

Many times in his Jersey City slum he had seen the police collar a presumed innocent black suspect just to say they had caught someone. The usual suspect, working the dope corner of course, was guilty of something for sure, but would certainly be convicted of whatever the latest offense charged. The local joke was that the prison was full of brothers serving each other's sentences.

Now poor Dave must have suffered a frighteningly long fall, probably falling right down on top of the real Ripper, and suffered a good beating there from the looks of him, and now an arrest for something he couldn't have done. Things just don't change; Bruno surmised sadly remembering his grandmother's admonition: "The black man has a tough road to hoe!"

Still Bruno didn't rush to put in his two cents to save Dave because he knew from experience that reason wouldn't work against the riled mob and would most certainly land big black Bruno himself in hot water too, so he opted to stay safe. Besides, from what he could see of Dave's face, Dave wasn't surprised about his as usual and oft expected plight. Wisely rationalizing the fearful logic of the cunning and deciding it was best that Dave have a friend on the outside Bruno silently stepped back and immersed himself in the growing, gleefully shouting crowd now wildly cheering about the Ripper's capture as though they personally had had a hand in it.

～～～～～

The harsh crackle hurt his eardrums as he, too late, pulled the phone away from his ear.

Clive fumed at the unexpected abruptness of the rebuff. Though not entirely surprising, her reaction still angered him. To be dumped is one thing, and doing the dumping not a new thing at that to Clive, but to be dumped himself first, and then to have the stinging venom of disdain turned his way for once, well that just wouldn't do. Clive thus plotted his revenge as the chauffer driven sedan cruised deeper into the foggy night.

"Pull over here Andy, I got a ping!" Clive suddenly shouted to his most unwilling driver, noting his solar watch glow red.

The Maybach sedan slid silently, in close to the curb and a tall figure stepped out of the shadows and entered the vehicle's rear.

Clive hadn't seen the fellow hiding in the shadows one bit and he bet the driver hadn't either.

The tall shadowy man lithely slid in onto the leather bench seat next to Clive, but far away on the far edge, not close at all. They both liked it that way; at arms, or pistol's length, as they both harbored no false illusions about their relationship's present parameters or ultimate and more than just possible violent ending.

The tall man doused the overhead lamp and adjusting his cowl and bowler downward over his net covered, grease paint darkened face, hugged the shadows inside the car as usual in his increasingly irritating way, Clive noticed. Clive was quite annoyed by the man disguising his true race, and also he imagined he could smell Morgan's trusty, bloody, foot and a half long blade stuck under his coat still dripping blood and it repulsed him all the more.

Clive hated Morgan, the "hypocritical bastard" as he privately referred to him, to be sure, but understood why the tall fellow with the misshapen face didn't want it seen head on. One side, the right side, of Morgan's twisted ugly face was long, gaunt, and narrow; the other, the left side was wide, soft, and puffy. Two truly ugly men poorly melded into one, Clive surmised snidely.

Despite his ugly appearance; happily, in their line of work, Morgan was proficient and deadly. And---you never used his name, never, not if you wanted to keep breathing, Clive earlier learned from his own handler.

"I did it. Oddly enough, that fellow Asher fell right out of the sky almost on top of me. You wouldn't know anything about that would you?" asked the tall man in a hoarse, raspy voice as he toweled the grease paint residue away from his face to reveal his natural ugliness.

"No, I don't. Is he alive?" Clive asked, snickering to himself.

"He was when I left him. I let him live. A red herring for the coppers I figured," rasped the man in the shadows, slyly lying.

Clive fumed inwardly anew. It would not serve his purpose to let this base fellow know that Clive had been most instrumental in Dave's dropping in on him, so Clive schemed nervously. But, how in the dickens had that black wanker survived the fall from the fifth floor? That vexing thought raced through Clive's mind as he struggled mightily to mask all his present concerns. In the future there would have to be better communication regarding their divergent activities' locations, to avoid overlapping, Clive resolved unhappily.

"Good idea, that'll give them fodder to chew on," Clive said cheerfully enough, he hoped, knowing that in the shadows the man was safely but avidly scrutinizing him all the while for outward signs of the hidden truth.

Morgan despised above all else, Clive's purposefully shaggy blond hair; his smooth Caucasian media propagandized handsome face, his undeserved position, his slick pastel colored sharkskin suits, and above all; his overly contrived upper-crust attitude. GOD's folly Morgan called it; putting such small, evil, stupid, worthless, talent-less people in supposedly attractive, perfectly functioning body shells while him, Morgan, who just oozed with intelligence, artistic talent, wit, and an abundance of superior character had to make do with a crude, ugly, misshapen body.

Morgan shuddered up and down the length of his long flanks with the happy anticipation of, soon, real soon he hoped, squeezing the fluids of life out of this future very, very unhandsome miscreant with his own gnarled bare hands.

"Drop me at Bright Gate, I've got to clean up, administer to my flock, and make preparations--- I'll bet," rasped the tall man obtusely offering up his over-sized open palm as usual for more payment.

~~~~~

Albion gave Dickett a look of total disgust, or was it pure envy? Dickett was in his middle fifties and he contained no enhanced organs or replacement parts at all in him; an anomaly, they called him jokingly, but not to his face. An original he was and rumor had it that his wife Claudia suffered the very same sad predicament.

Unlike Albion with his heart pacemaker and new liver, Dickett somehow made do with his original parts to everyone else's consternation and jealous gossip. Even Sergeant Craig Oliver; with his new genetically engineered blue eyes and genetically rearranged brain in order to at long last, think and live a straight man's life like a real straight man, childishly derided Dickett and other originals.

"You can see the trail as plain as I can," Dickett stated dully, pointing out the blood trail leading from the street to the slowly opening manhole being manhandled by police robots.

Albion lifted the sheet and saw what was left of a once pretty woman. The sight caused him to shudder.

"Who was she?" Albion asked.

"Trinny Simpson, sophomore street walker," Dickett responded patting his left chest discretely.

Albion nodded in the negative and walked over to the now open manhole.

Buster, the unhappy German Shepard chosen for the task at hand, was being lowered down into the manhole by pulley and harness by his human handlers and his and Albion's eyes met momentarily in a sad moment of true brotherhood and doomed understanding for both.

"Blood trail leads down just as our lone witness; Asher's statement infers. He was thrown out that window up there," Dickett reported, pointing upwards.

"What's that?" Albion asked pointing to a shard of long twisted silver metal at Dickett's feet.

"I don't know, simple trash I reckon. It looks like it came out of one of these trash bags," Dickett answered, puzzled.

"Bag it for me, and don't include it with the stuff they picked up here, you hear? I want to get my own scan by Billingsly. I'm suddenly getting an idea," Albion quipped with the growing satisfaction of discovering something he was sure would take his present deductions away from the paranormal and into the realm of the far more normal criminal happenings; that is if what he suspected was right.

"We caught another one of the skinheads!" Dickett chuckled proudly.

"Where is he?" Albion asked, his spirits picking up a bit more.

"Right over here. We found him laid out in the stairwell of the Carlton Arms Hotel," Dickett said leading Albion over to the meat wagon which he opened with a flourish to reveal his unexpected catch of the night.

Inside sprawled a shackled, thin, battered, bleeding fellow looking back out with one good eye. It was obvious that someone had gone over him real hard in their interrogation, but Albion didn't care to find out whom.

"Name?" Albion asked, gingerly crawling in.

"His name's Vince Sewell, we found him in the stairwell---like that," Dickett answered smiling sheepishly, holding the wagon door open.

"I asked him!" Albion, disbelieving Dickett's disclaimer of no assault, snapped.

Albion, sneered now at the unresponsive Vince Sewell, all the while nervously pulling on his rubber gloves.

"I asked you a question!" shouted Albion to the fellow cowering in the wagon. Albion slyly slipped on his brass knuckles over his rubber gloved right hand as he climbed up into the wagon.

"I ain't saying nothing more. I want me a solicitor!" the fellow cried back defiantly.

Albion short sucker punched the hapless fellow square in his nose sending him sprawling back hard against the floor.

"We'll see," Albion growled ominously, slowly advancing on the hapless fellow.

Dickett discretely closed the wagon door behind his boss, leaving it a bit ajar for his own twisted visual amusement and to safeguard his boss's safety.

~~~~~

Dave briskly rubbed his wrists where the just released shackles had rubbed roughly into his skin and regarded warily the three policemen avidly conversing among themselves over in the far corner.

After a stop at the hospital for more poking, gluing, and prodding, this time by a real human, they had brought him over here inside New Scotland Yard for interrogation. The interrogation room he was sitting in was the standard one as seen on many detective TV shows. The usual; in the middle of the floor table, where he sat behind on a hard chair, and of course the requisite two-way mirrors hung on the opposing far walls.

Dave's torn clothes reeked of blood and garbage and he knew that if he smelled himself then others were having a hard time hanging around him too. Too bad for the police, he snickered. His once, this morning's fashionable bamboo bush jacket now hung on him in smelly tatters. Dave wondered, as he figured all similarly held prisoners had; who was watching me from behind those mirrors.

The over head light added insult to injury by hotly burning a hole in the top of his hung head.

The three cops appeared to be arguing over his statement that he had given their pod. This had to be his very lowest point in life, Dave reasoned sadly. His guilt at being the long sought ripper a foregone conclusion to the policemen; they had relished every indignity they had heaped on him during the last two hours of his interrogation.

Oddly, surreally, this presently degrading experience reminded Dave of something similar in his past.

Once long ago on a lazy stormy night while in college in Philadelphia he'd faced three desperate fellow classmates across a chessboard. He had beaten them all individually and taken their money. Now desperate to regain their cash; they were playing as one mind with benefit of a chess book all the while plying Dave with whiskey and reefers. Inexorably they were pushing the intoxicated Dave back across the board until he luckily experienced an epiphany and realized how funny it was that it took them and all this to beat him. With that realization Dave smiled and hunkered down and as drunk and high as he was; still in the end he soon turned the tables on his outnumbering foes and vanquished the surprised trio against all the odds against him.

That unexpected inner resolve now unexpectedly filled Dave's soul up and he hunkered down into his inner self again to get ready to beat whatever was coming next.

The door suddenly flew open and in walked Inspector Albion behind a lividly ruddy faced, busty English woman even larger than him. The large, boisterous, corpulent woman dressed in black from bowler's head to shiny pointy shoe shod toe briskly offered up her card to the instantly stunned Dave.

"I'm Nigela Salty of Needleman, Beedleman, Candy, Stein, and Salty, solicitors. I've been retained to represent you!" she bellowed to the totally flabbergasted Dave.

"My client has been assaulted by persons unknown, thrown out a window, and now detained unlawfully by you! I will expect your report regarding your investigation into my client's assault soon, or I'll make a complaint to the King's review! Do I make myself clear?" Salty threatened Albion in a blustery tone that even Dave knew meant serious business.

"I have here a writ of habeas corpus and I and my client are leaving!" Salty now shouted at Albion who hardly hid his red-faced consternation at the writ being roughly thrust into his chest.

"Come on lad, we're leaving. Don't say another word to them. They don't have anything on you anyway," Salty advised, grabbing Dave by the arm and pulling him out of the room quite roughly.

Dave passed Albion who remarked, "Anytime you want to talk lad, you have my number."

"My client is not a suspect as you well know. He's a material witness at best, and when you're ready to play fair I'll accept inquiries. No more statements Albion, you know the rules!" Salty barked as she herded Dave along past Albion and a whole slew of glowering policemen massing in the hall in a makeshift gauntlet of serious interest.

Salty rushed Dave out of the building and into her waiting transport; a new, pewter colored Electric Rolls.

Tumbling into the back seat Dave now paused to finally notice the lady for what she was; a big-moneyed powerful, competent, mouthpiece, quite used to the criminal trade and their large fees. Her name was quite an apt description for her bravado and bluster. Salty pulled out a large Havana cheroot and proceeded to blur her baggy green eyes and round, ruddy features behind the pungent smoke with no apparent regard for the driver or Dave.

The limousine started up and merged with the traffic with a smooth whisper of a swoosh of its Clowder fitted electric turbine engine.

"Here's your property," Salty said pulling out a large manila envelope from under her black, ample breast-bulging cashmere overcoat, "they can't keep it."

"Where are we going?" Dave asked waving away Salty's smoke from his vision and wondering how in the world they had invented non-toxic tobacco while still retaining such thick smoke.

"You're going to your hotel. I've persuaded the Carlton Arms to pony up a much better room for you on a semi-permanent basis, at no charge to you since you were assaulted on their premises and I, no, you're seeking significant damages. I reckoned you fancied a shower and a shave, and a rest. I on the other hand have much more work to do on your behalf yet," Salty crowed, "I've also applied to get your visa extended on behalf of your benefactor."

"I almost forgot. Here, this is a credit card. The limit is a thousand £ pounds, remember that. From your looks and smell you sure need a change of attire---bad!" Salty laughed, gingerly handing said item over to Dave.

"I can't thank Ziv enough," Dave said happily, pulling out his cell phone and wallet from the police envelope.

"Ziv? Ziv? who's Ziv?" Salty lazily asked from somewhere under her heady smoke screen.

"Ziv Finkel of Image Retrieval. My boss. Didn't he retain you?" Dave asked cautiously.

"Never heard of him. Another party who wishes to maintain their anonymity retained me," Salty puffed on.

Dave, now totally confused and wondering if he had fell out of one frying pan into another fire, accessed the lone message on his phone and was at once quite sure that Salty was telling the truth.

The message read: "We sent you over there to catch an event, not to start an international incident and become a shit smear on this company! You're fired! Ziv."

Chapter 5

Wednesday, October 5, 2016

Friar Evan Morgan reached up and grabbing the old tattered hemp rope with his unusually long hairy arms he tugged again for all he was worth. His vigorous efforts pulled the bell rope down hard and the tower bell sixty feet above him again resounded with a loud ominous, hollow clang, pulling him up off the ground on the upswing. He loved this above all; the simple tasks like calling the faithful to worship or in this case: breakfast.

With the bell tolling on its own above him, and the faithful below scurrying to eat, Morgan released the rope and adjusted his cowl over the bane of his existence; his head.

"Thank GOD for Bright Gate for giving me an outlet for my higher aspirations, and thank GOD for the present corrupt government for giving me an equally opportune outlet for my baser drives," he thought aloud as he hurried down to join his brothers and acolytes at breakfast, by gingerly taking the medieval era winding bell tower staircase down.

Once in the great hall he took his place at the great ancient long oak table against the north wall facing horizontally before the ten hungry acolyte filled tables in the room. His seat was left, three removed from the center; the head friar's seat, and as he settled in on the hard wood bench seat he listened to the morning's prayer with much interest.

The subject this morning was the forgiveness of our sins and Morgan felt deeply that this sermon was meant for him above all others in the room.

By day he toiled in the abbey's monastery as a good friar, doing whatever tasks assigned, on sabbatical and often by night, on special occasions, he did the bidding of the bosses in the government's back rooms. At first he rationalized his doing evil for them as solving his need for money, but as time went on he realized that their seedy jobs served to sate his dual personality's insatiable need to hurt and maim; to get back at society for his misshapen, crooked, ugly face, body, and demeanor hidden under his monk's brown hooded robe.

The fact that he had been in the government's employ as an assassin long before he helped create Bright Gate seeking his own personal salvation didn't give him much succor this morning as he was still unsuccessfully seeking said salvation with very little success. He'd certainly tried, tried hard and harder as time went on, he remembered sadly, but the call of the wild always beckoned and its evil call always won out over his higher aspirations.

Now he simply barely tolerated his warring dual traits with a sense of quiet, peaceful coexistence if not a happy inner satisfaction.

～～～～～

Dave sat uncomfortably in the large tufted brown leather armchair warily watching his "benefactor" busily toil over his liquid helix laptop.

Salty had roused him from his first peaceful sleep in days early this morning to whisk him over here, where ever that was, to meet the one who had bailed him out of custody. Salty's Rolls carried them out of the dark, fog shrouded city and deep out into the beautifully clear blue skies and rolling countryside using every winding road possible, Dave thought, to a nondescript, thatched roof of a country cottage building; then down an unexpected long ramp a few floors to this place.

Then they came down a long elevator shaft to this very large room Salty led and then left him while she sexily pandered to the two large black guards outside.

The room was at least thirty feet by thirty feet with blue concrete walls even higher. A lone curved dark mahogany desk sat in the middle of the room with a lone arm chair sitting before it. On three of the walls facing outward from the desk hung massive LCD screens, on the fourth behind the desk hung a large colorful painting of some kind of bloody, titanic struggle.

Dave sadly watched the LCD high above and behind his benefactor and saw the news broadcast, the fallout from the ill-advised, petulant, prestidigitation driven global politics of the early 2000's: "Mid-East wide Sunni versus Shiite Civil wars now in tenth year!....Arab Coalition vows revenge against latest U.S. led invasion of Syria!......U.N. study shows Iraq now the capital of world-wide terrorist movement!....North Korean surface ships clash with those of the Japanese navy!......Tsunami hits Australia!......Egypt goes on the offensive against Jihadist invasion!....U.S. invades Chile!"

Luckily waking early had given Dave the opportunity to see Bruno before his departing for the States; plainly shackled down with the Extraminator's silver case. Ziv wasted little time or money, and summarily ordered the immediate return of Bruno and the Extraminator home.

They met in the lobby as Bruno hurried out to catch his return jet. Dave had decided last night while lying in his sumptuous hotel bed to stay in London a while and rest and live off the largess of the hotel; while it lasted, since he didn't have any hot prospects back home. Their parting meeting was far shorter and emotionally gut wrenching than either had reason to expect, still they had promised to meet at the Ben Franklin Hotel in Philly for drinks soon.

Dave wasn't overly surprised as he watched the man toiling busily before him to find that Benjamin Cresasern, his "benefactor", was the one he owed his freedom to.

Cresasern explained as Dave entered, leaving Salty outside that he was in the middle of tabulating his thousands of his employee's lottery results regarding future corporate courses of action. He stated that he found the lottery to be more precise at predicting the future than had any super computer's prognostications been.

Dave watched the solidly built, bald man work hard, dwarfed by the large office with its imposingly high walls and wondered nervously what the powerful, rich man wanted from him that he didn't already have.

"Sorry to keep you stewing but I had to complete that before I knew what to do with you," Cresasern finally explained, looking up.

"What to do with me?" Dave echoed, as concern and confusion began growing in his mind.

"You've done us a good turn, and I hope you'll do us another," Cresasern said, eyeing Dave ominously.

"I don't know what you're talking about," Dave answered naively.

"I owe you an explanation. The mini-dot we scanned off of you was stolen information; stolen by parties unknown, from us. They stole our detailed secret plans, partner lists, long range objectives, system protocols, everything. Luckily our team retrieved them back before delivery to whomever at extreme cost to the five people sent out. The last surviving one; Sidney Mellors planted the dot on you before he was killed," Cresasern said sullenly.

"Why all the fuss?" Dave asked, not hiding that he was totally lost in all this intrigue.

"We've beat them at their own game. We've totally disrupted their monopolies; we've cut them out of owning production, distribution, and total control of the consumer markets in the energy fields. The only intelligent course they have left is to steal our plans and leapfrog over us and in effect become us in order to once again control the pace of progress and thus keep the money flowing back into their pockets," Cresasern said seriously.

"We?" Dave asked, smugly thinking he knew fully well who "we" and "them" was.

"We're a small, but rapidly growing, part of a new world capitalist market phenomenon; they call us the disrupters, a direct offshoot of the vigorous application of Black Science. Ever hear of us?" Cresasern asked.

"Can't say as I have," Dave answered back.

"Our mantra is free market progress. We refuse to let the old boy monopolies control world markets; once they get too big they stop thinking, they stop competition and progress, and economies of consumer prices, that's why G.M. and Ford had to merge. That's why there was no competition in the world's oil business. Why compete when you run the show? The only things they want are controlled costs, rising prices, and no upstarts with new technology disrupting their monetary strangleholds on us all. We intend to disrupt them forever!" Cresasern stated flatly.

Cresasern rose and came over closer to Dave and stood towering over him somewhat menacingly.

"I want to offer you a job, at approximately double what Image Retrieval paid you!" Cresasern suddenly barked, leaning back to sit on the edge of his desk.

"Doing what?" Dave answered warily, totally surprised now.

"As a front: ostensibly as our corporate news correspondent here in Britain, in actuality; as a catcher for us. We want to know what or who is behind the Ripper killings, and since "they" obviously have you in their sights already you're a sure bet for us to get somewhere in finding out. We want to know the whys and wherefores of the recent move to discredit Black Science. That is if you aren't afraid?" Cresasern warned, smiling.

Dave could only stare back at the man before him since he hadn't a clue up to now what the fellow wanted.

"You didn't think it was only about you, did you?" Cresasern asked abruptly.

"No, but after all I've been through I'm past afraid at this point. Still I'd love to get to the bottom of this but I can't see as how that's possible. The Extraminator is illegal over here, if I'm caught using it I'd be locked up, or worse---again," Dave said shaking his head negatively and warily.

"We swab your cheek for DNA and your body's unique mixture of minerals and elements which we use to construct a genetically engineered electro-biological, chemical, miniature Extraminator; a thin, small patch way less than an inch square by an inch in size, which we place right behind your eye ball, left or right; whichever our doctors finds most suitable. It's motivated by you mentally and, it's totally undetectable to scanners--- so far," Cresasern stated matter-of-factly.

Dave blinked hard in growing total disbelief.

"All I know is that its nano-technology, something new and exciting happening on a daily basis. I've had one in me for the last year," Cresasern crowed, "It doesn't hurt a bit; in fact you'll never know it's in there. It will take nearly a week or to learn how to use it correctly though."

Dave still didn't believe his ears, but the man before him appeared to be dead serious.

"Make no mistake son, this is dangerous work, many people have been killed, on both sides in this war, and that's certainly what it is, and since they've already made an attempt on your life you should assume they certainly will again. Don't decide lightly," Cresasern warned ominously.

Dave swallowed in a loud gulp.

"To accept my offer all you have to do is write down on this paper what my man Mellors spoke to you before they killed him. In return you get the job and this," Cresasern said dramatically holding up a piece of folded paper in his right hand while pointing with the left to the pad and pen on his desk.

Dave hesitated, totally surprised and confused.

"Why do you need that?" Dave asked, vainly trying to digest the import of all of what he was hearing.

"Mellors wasn't sure that he'd make it back alive so he added some really incriminating information about our enemies and an encoded code to the dot disk. Using a password extractor or the incorrect password will cause the disk to self-destruct, thus we need the password," Cresasern explained.

"What incriminating information?" Dave asked.

"That's classified and my concern son, suffice to say you'll be doing us a good turn again.--- Or you can go back to the States where no one would hire you for even a dogcatcher's job once Image Retrieval gets finished dissing you," Cresasern jibed knowingly.

"What's that?" Dave finally asked referring to the folded paper Cresasern still proffered up ominously.

"It's the G.P.S. coordinates and exact time coordinates of the time you as a newborn were placed on that park bench in Rittenhouse Square Park in Philadelphia!" Cresasern said tersely with a strange sad glint in his eye.

~~~~~

Heda, using her liquid helix computer, eagerly perused the various airline manifests looking for that which she wondered why in the world she was looking for in the first place. She found Bruno Guntz's scheduled flight but there was no mention of a Dave Asher anywhere leaving Great Britain even on omnibus search farther in the future.

The floor's service robot interrupted her. With the face of Margaret Thatcher pasted on its head by some BBC prankster it silently rolled in and dropped off the morning's mail without much ado and promptly split.

"You're not listening to me," intoned the sweetly raspy voice coming from the chair in the corner of the suddenly all too smallish fully glassed-in-cubicle.

So true, she thought as she ignored the incessant, ongoing, pointless, mutterings of her uninvited guest as usual.

"If you're going to ignore me I'll just leave," they rasped sadly.

Heda stared bleakly at the softly flickering three dimensional holographic image of her mother sitting over in the corner knitting and pouting as usual and Heda hated science all the more for this latest curse. "Oh for the old days of the mundane land-line telephone," she groaned to herself.

"You know I'm working mom, why don't you show up at my flat at a decent hour like most people?" Heda asked the image, quite exasperated.

"I don't like the vibe there since you took up with that last one; that spawn of the devil Clive, you know very well," her mother snapped back.

"I dumped him long ago!" Heda retorted, becoming more flustered and exhaling loudly.

"Still, his evil karma is still there, I can smell it," mom continued irritatingly.

"Impossible!" snapped Heda.

"That's what you think, and we both know how bad your mental reasoning can be," mom nagged even more smugly.

"If it wasn't for me you'd never caught him fooling around on you," mom chuntered on.

"I got work to do!" Heda barked.

"Doesn't look that way to me! Are you still on ice?" mom asked nosily.

"That's it! Goodbye!" Heda snapped and hit the virtual video termination button on her desk causing her mother's vexed image to abruptly flicker anew and spiral out of focus into nothingness.

What a relief, Heda thought as she found herself free from her mother's usual prying and snide innuendoes alone in her office. Still her mother had been right. After the Bernier Street Ripper fiasco the BBC now relegated her to desk duties only, for how long; that's the question.

Luckily they hadn't broadcast live that fateful night or there would be a much worse panic all over the island, she happily reasoned.

~~~~~

Friday, October, 7, 2016

Clive sweated profusely. He respectfully walked a bit behind the anti-magnetically operated floating wheelchair listening to the loud, angry railing of its occupant.

"How in the hell are you going to rise if you continue using a hammer to bang on an atom! Don't you have any sense? You're a great disappointment to the privy council and especially to me!" shouted Sir Reginald Bowden, Clive's handler in the Ministry.

"Waddell, I try to raise you up a class and you try to go down two!" Sir Reginald screamed on.

Clive took his harangue as usual with little emotion showing as he slyly glanced down on the growing bald spot on top of the old, gray haired, bushy eye browed, crippled, reprobate's odd shaped head, reaming him out once again.

"All you had to do was to hire a few professional thugs and waylay that black wanker discreetly. Instead you hire every idiotic aspiring Nazi in East London, and still you don't get the job done. If you possessed any sense you'd have spent half of the cash on proper thugs and pocketed the rest like a real upper crust gentleman of our party would! All that money wasted!" Sir Reginald went on loudly, his grey eyes gleaming dully.

Clive rushed ahead and opened the door leading into Sir Reginald's office for the old slaphead codger in his best most subservient, servile way.

Inside the cavernous office Clive once again felt his breath being taken away. The richly furnished room simply oozed the aura of old world opulence, excessive sumptuousness, and the blatant ostentation of old money and a lot of it.

"By now that bastard Cresasern will have retrieved his property---! Still I want that Asher character for a little interrogation! Bring him out to the farm ASAP and ring me up!" Sir Reginald barked floating easily over behind his desk with an oft practiced suaveness.

Clive simply watched and waited, still awed by the largess surrounding him and his myriad racing desires and serpentine plots to acquire some of same.

"This time use Fred and Andy only, I want this done correctly! No more Nazi trash you hear? If you don't do this right your head is going to sorely miss your body!" Sir Reginald warned, glowering at Clive and flying from behind the desk softly floating back and forth in an easy lazy manner like a pendulum.

Clive bowed low in well practiced acceptance of his present position.

"Here is the next victim for Morgan, have him do it next week, at least this part of the plan is on schedule," Sir Reginald said throwing a rolled up package at Clive who caught it deftly with his right hand.

Leaving, Clive took a look into the package past the money at the papers within and wasn't surprised at the name enclosed.

For some time he had suspected an alternate agenda to Sir Reginald's hit list, and the proof lay before him. The name had appeared on the "telly" last week in connection with a dispute between Sir Reginald's development company and a bunch of soon to be displaced locals.

Sir Reginald had often told Clive that they were doing this on orders from far higher up the command chain to discredit Black Science and somehow or other regain their rightful access to their unlawfully lost power and missing cash flows but the sick reality of this dirty business had struck Clive hard, long ago.

This whole sordid scheme was purely personal, not tied to officially mandated powers at all, just a personal criminal enterprise of Sir Reginald and his cronies, Clive was well certain now.

~~~~~

Sunday, October 9, 2016

Albion twisted uncomfortably in his rigid hospital bed. His chest itched something fierce, and would continue to, since he adamantly eschewed the often offered pain killers since his transplant operation two days ago.

"Florence, why don't you go home? I don't think I'm about to die today," Albion said with a wan smile to the long suffering woman half a sleep sitting near his bed.

"Just my luck, I just paid the premium," Florence joked sleepily, pulling her fur tighter over her ample, buxom form.

"Go on old girl, I'll be home tomorrow anyway," Albion entreated his wife.

"I think I will go down to get a bite, but I'll be back," she cooed kissing his wrinkled brow with an unexpected but seemingly genuine loving sentiment.

Watching her still handsome figure leave, Albion wondered what he had done to deserve her. He was no angel. He kept late hours. He was rude, inconsiderate, inattentive, and bull-headed, yet she'd always stood by him. He wondered why.

"How's it going chief? I just saw Florence leave," Harry Dickett said as he cautiously came into the room. He was clutching under his arm a newspaper and a large manila envelope and Albion knew that he was in for it now.

"As well as can be expected of a man with a new heart, and I fear a new much better, more humane view on a very seedy life," Albion said snidely.

"Are you kidding?" asked Dickett looking about nervously.

"Did she see you?" Albion queried his most unwilling partner-in-crime.

"No I hid like a school kid. Expecting her back soon?" Dickett asked feigning fear and suspicion.

"No and nobody else is here now. Quick before that doctor returns; what have you got?" Albion asked eagerly gesturing for Dickett's package.

"The paper and photos! They don't know I copied the photos! I think we have a copycat murderer!" Dickett crowed.

Albion perused the Evening Standard newspaper first and discovered that the story was shocking and to the point: The latest victim; Vince Sewell was found gutted early last night in Whitechapel with no note left by the suspected Ripper on the victim, a deviation from the prior murders.

The paper went to say that a bloodstained note, along with one of Vince Sewell's more odiously inked severed tattoos was sent to the editor later, saying:

"Sir Boss,

I tender to you this faker. Let the other fakers know that I am coming to get them next. Thus die all pretenders to my quest! Signed: ---Jack----."

The gory photos confirmed to Albion that it might well be the same fellow's work.

"Vince Sewell---? I know that one. We brought him in last week after I "interrogated" him!" Albion gasped.

"Good riddance to bad rubbish. Still this casts a new, scary shadow on the case, to some far more than others," Dickett smirked.

"What's all this about?" Doctor Clarence Everett suddenly boomed startling the two men in the room.

Lost in their unauthorized work they hadn't heard him enter.

Papers and photos went scattering about as Dickett sheepishly hustled and scrambled to retrieve his stuff scattered on the floor.

"I told you no work until I tell you!" Doctor Everett shouted to Albion as Dickett took the hint and exited quickly.

Doctor Everett took Albion's pulse and found it highly elevated.

"Are you trying to kill yourself?" the doctor asked, as he attacked Albion's newly scarred chest with a cold stethoscope, unknowingly stepping on a photo accidentally left by Dickett.

Albion simply shrugged but the thought of that poor sap Vince Sewell being hacked up troubled him. All along his experience had led him to suspect some fakery afoot for some unknown party's purpose in the murders. The thought that perhaps, no matter how weird it seemed, that now a copycat with their own sick agenda or even worse; the real Jack the Ripper might be on the scene sent a shiver up his spine and caused his pulse rate to spike anew.

~~~~~

Wednesday, October 12, 2016

Morgan had waited nearly motionless in the dark for the last fifteen minutes. Thoughts of unseen demons lurking threateningly in the dark uncharacteristically played on his nerves this night and made the time seen to last forever. He wondered if this new sensation was one that he had never felt before; that is fear.

He didn't have long to wait though, as he suddenly heard the door open and a short, rotund male figure entered the darkened room and went straight for the light switch.

Morgan smiled evilly as he crisply made his move. The fellow switched the light switch once, twice to no avail.

Morgan knew the switch wouldn't work since he had pulled the fuses earlier upon entering through the basement of the fenced-in town house.

Coming up silently behind the fumbling fellow and grabbing him around the mouth with his left hand, Morgan stuck his foot and a half long serrated blade deep, real deep, into the hapless man's back silently with one powerful thrust.

The man grunted and sagged back down against Morgan immediately, and Morgan felt the force of life flee the punctured body in a single gasp under his gloved hand.

Holding his victim fast to prevent a noisy fall Morgan lowered the man to the floor, where he proceeded to follow instructions as to the exact way to butcher him.

Shaky hands and his nervously peering about into the surrounding dark caused the odious work to go slower than usual in the dark, since Morgan didn't dare use more than his own laser light wrapped around his ear.

Once done with his present grisly task, and taking his requested souvenir, he pinned the enclosed note to the corpse's bloody lapel and dragged the man out the door, leaving quite a prominent red blood trail behind, as instructed, and sprawled him out splayed prominently under the grey glow of the overhead winking crescent moon on the walkway in front of the large Redbridge borough town house, once again, as instructed.

His never before felt trepidation this night he traced right back to that fop; Clive, as his mind raced back to earlier this night.

"What's the meaning of this? Are you angling for something, perhaps a bit more dosh?" Clive screamed as he threw the newspaper at Morgan.

They were in the speeding Maybach with Clive's two surly henchmen in the front seat sitting as silent as church mice. No doubt stewing on the folly of their own twisted, unrealized, dreams, Morgan figured.

Glancing closely at the troubling headline which Clive indicated, caused an uncharacteristic cold shiver to run up Morgan's spine as he took in the entire gist and prescribed conclusions of the article.

The Evening Standard article read: "Real Jack The Ripper On The Hunt For His Imposters. One Already Slain!"

"I don't know anything about this!" Morgan angrily shouted back.

"Right!" snapped Clive, not believing him at all.

"Looks like we all had better watch our backs, especially you Clive; Sewell was one of yours," Morgan said somberly, feeling the night's cold air suddenly enter and swirl around and rudely touch each of the car's inhabitants to a man.

Chapter 6

Saturday, October 15, 2016

Dave sheepishly but blatantly watched the young, attractive couple's vigorously heated twistings on his hotel's bed as they made passionate love; and not that long ago by his eye screen's digital reckoning.

He could tell that they had feelings for each other and he felt ashamed to watch, but still he did. He chalked this particular indiscretion of his up to his growing horniness and a natural healthy prurient interest. It had been a long time since he and Olivia had done anything almost like that and Dave knew they probably never would again since she still refused his calls as she had done since he'd been in England. That sense of loss served as his moral rationalization this morning, but not too well.

Suddenly the vision of the lovely, aloof, cold, brown doe eyed, snarling, Heda Marish came into his artificially excited mind and he wondered why.

"Stop that---!" loudly boomed in his ear.

Reluctantly stopping the implanted Extraminator's replay with a mere thought, Dave listened in to his earpiece, quite embarrassed by the abruptness of the bust.

"Its working fine, you can stop doing stupid things now!" Cresasaern barked in Dave's ear.

Earlier, after breakfast, Dave stood across the street from the Carlton Arms Hotel on Watling Street and, as a test; he began using his implant's control of: scan, and live replay, and had watched the hotel's actual construction brick by brick in 1905 backwards and then forwards, twice. Both times his inconspicuous, unfelt implanted device performed flawlessly and also by his mental command, sent Cresasern the ongoing video by way of uplink.

Turning his device back even farther in time until his eye screen read 64 A.D. Dave panned around in a full arc and beheld many Roman soldiers and original scruffy Britons, meandering about in their usual activities in the area for over an hour. Looking west far up the steep hill of Watling Street north of the hotel yielded the sight of an old Roman fort's wooden ramparts at Cripplegate and the small squalid thatched British hutted town far below.

Scanning about through the past of the now bustling modern city streets showed mostly a vast expanse of ancient empty countryside dotted here and there with toiling farmers in the fields. Focusing northward a block Dave beheld the wooden Roman bridge built in 32 A.D. spanning the Thames River just a block away from the present London Bridge and a good number of locals moving about.

Watching the two bridges existing simultaneously; thus Dave suddenly encountered Cresasern's admonition regarding something he called "bi-lateral vision". By playing back live, in real "now time", the visions of the past Dave suffered the troubling experience of living and acting in two time zones simultaneously. While walking the streets as he beheld visions of the now and the past simultaneously overlapping each other Dave felt the confusion Cresasern described. In plain language Dave didn't know easily who to get out of the way of; the real people walking around now or the past people concurrently bustling to and fro also.

Solving the quandary was simple; just turn down the contrast on the replay; thus rendering the past visions of people, things, and places as transparent as required to discern the presently real from the past. This done; Dave could now enjoy the experience much better.

"What a rush! What a rush!" he echoed as he became more adept at controlling his new toy.

And the entire experience and past scenes he found fascinating because the inhabitants; they all seemed so serious and sullen, and he didn't want to stop watching but the need for lunch beckoned stronger and sooner than expected.

The hotel restaurant was quite good and free to Dave so he made it a point to eat there as much as possible.

While munching his latest free meal he saw the restaurant's overhead news ticker spouting the latest news: "L.A. traffic shutdown forced due to build up of air pollution from China!.....Tanning salons banned in U.S. due to skin cancer epidemic!....Oak tree bark derived herpes cure in final trials!.....Dauntless space probe docks at space station Alpha-2 with suspected live spores from Saturn's moon Enceladus!"

"Mind if I take the rest of the day off? It is Saturday," Dave asked into his ear speaker phone between bites of salad.

"Sure son, just keep the line open," Cresasern answered, "what's your plan sport?"

"A bit of sightseeing, watching the birds. You know, you were young once, right?"

"Just keep the line open!" snapped Cresasern.

Cresasern now appeared to be the closest thing Dave had to a friend. The fellow employed him, fronted him money, offered advice, and had implanted the most wondrous device into his head. What a strange relationship, Dave laughed. Writing down the word "Zither81" or so it sounded at the airport, hadn't been as hard a task as Dave had expected. And why not, Cresasern was the only one not trying to kill him lately? ---At least not yet? Dave surmised drolly.

Walking the bustling streets without causing any untoward attention lately to be called to him, Dave found exhilarating.

Taking in the British museum, Dave soon found himself before a glass case containing metal armor once worn by ancient to medieval warriors. His reflection in the glass didn't hide the fact that the armor all appeared to be too small for him, especially the helmets. Now Dave considered his six foot frame short, but seeing these old things hanging empty before him he knew at once that he would have been considered a burly, tall man in those past times, and so he left the museum smiling.

The London populace had moved on from recognizing him as at the worst; "The Ripper" or "that fellow that brought Black Science to kill us", to them not recognizing him at all and he loved it. To blend and interact with fellow humans without their fearful glances or sneers was a happy occurrence for him to be savored and enjoyed to the max, Dave felt. He spent half the day doing this simple thing and blended into the bustling crowd downtown with none of the locals the wiser enjoying his new found anonymity as much or more than he ever expected he would.

The locals ran here and there with their phones plastered to their ears lost in their own silly machinations to Dave's glee. Not a second look was sent his way from the hurried London pedestrians as he finally, slowly sauntered over toward Trafalgar Square.

Walking around the square as evening started, Dave spied an open air bar across on the north side and sitting there he couldn't believe his eyes who he saw sitting and sipping there. Working up his nerve he approached and soon stood above his object of interest this day.

"Well, isn't it a small world?" Dave said, feeling stupid using such a worn line.

The two young women looked up in practiced unison at him and reflexively gave him the well-honed icy sneering look they reserved for wolves on the make saying silently, but loudly, "get lost squirrel!"

Dave read the sign well and stepped back ready for polite flight.

Heda suddenly recognized Dave and her attitude changed immediately; the ice turned warm, and giving her friend but a knowing glance said silently to her at least a thousand unspoken words in "womenspeak."

To Dave she said jokingly, even cracking a smile of sorts while she did it, "I thought you were deported."

"Not me. I even have a straight job now. May I join you?" Dave asked, looking at the two fierce damsels most pleadingly.

"I guess so. That if Joyce here doesn't mind," Heda said cattily.

"Joyce this is Dave, Dave this is Joyce. I told you about him, didn't I?" Heda asked, still smiling oddly, why Dave didn't know, but it bothered him.

"Where are you working now? I heard you and Image Retrieval parted company," Heda said knowingly.

"The Cresasern Group, I'm in their public relations department," Dave stated this succinctly but with an obvious new air of boasting.

Heda's eyes and ears perked up at that unexpected news.

The two shapely, leggy, pretty, sophisticated looking, olive-skinned women were a beautiful sight to Dave as he grabbed a chair. Both were dressed in short skirts, brightly colored semi-revealing tops and jackets and looked really fine. Heda wore her long reddish black hair down to her shoulders and it fairly shined a deep purple in the afternoon Sun with a luster that was becoming more mesmerizing to Dave as he watched. Her sharp Asian features positively captivated Dave provocatively to the point that he struggled not to stare at her too much. The fact that she was showing a bit of honest cleavage didn't escape his notice either.

"Can I get you ladies a drink since I'm newly solvent?" Dave asked suavely, he hoped.

"I really must go. I have to see a woman about a cat. I'll take a rain check, nice to meet you," Joyce suddenly said as she rose; a knowing smirk aimed at Heda quickly passing over her pert face, unseen by Dave.

Heda didn't miss the fact that Dave rose as Joyce did. Old world, mannered, gentlemen were as scarce as hen's teeth in present day London at least in her circles, she bemoaned silently.

With Joyce gone, Dave was left nervously sitting with Heda straight across from him, who eyed him strangely as though she was waiting for him to pull a rabbit out of his hat.

Actually she was watching his sparkling light brown eyes in well hidden joy since she had fretted his fate for nearly the last fortnight. Dave felt the unease grow in him along with the growing, exciting sheer pleasure of being alone with her for the first time.

"Cat got your tongue?" she snapped at once as the waiter brought over two gin and tonics.

Dave was shocked out of his mindless stupor and smiled, and stammered, "No, I'm just speechless; I didn't expect to see you again."

Well I'm still here, it appears," Heda said sarcastically.

"You're not making this easy, have a bit of pity for an awe struck admirer," Dave begged sheepishly.

"Okay, let's start over. You never know, we may turn out to be friends," she said smiling openly and offering her hand over the table.

"Fine by me," Dave returned cheerily as he took her soft cool hand in his and he felt a jolt hit him and course through his entire body with an electrical shock of frightening proportions.

~~~~~

Albion slowly, thoughtfully, arranged his two blackboards in front of his captive morning roll call audience, all the while secreting a rolled up report regarding the silver metal shard he'd taken at the Trinny Simpson murder scene just received from Professor Billingsly into his jacket pocket.

On the left board he placed the three Berner Street dead victims' names, and time, annotated pictures up in the top left side corner. Beside and to the right of them he placed particulars on Elbert Stoner, Trinny Simpson, and last night's victim; Sir Arthur Claypool along with copies of Jack's grisly notes.

On the right blackboard he placed Vince Sewell's mug shot; all alone with the note sent to the paper.

The policemen, he knew watching him this morning weren't at all buying his argument.

"These folks on my right were killed by the original perpetrator, calling himself Jack. He sends me notes like he knows me," Albion said slapping the blackboard hard with his pointer.

"The one on my left was killed by the new guy in town; I call him "Mr. Unknown". He sends his notes to the Evening Standard paper, which has identified him as a bona fide demon calling himself the real Jack. I don't think he knows me I'm quite sure!" Albion cried, while facing the throng and pointing each blackboard's contents out with a strong arm flourish he hadn't been able to muster prior to his transplant.

The uniformed mob of police sitting before him shifted uncomfortably in their seats waiting for the first brave one to dissent. That one would be the sacrifice to Albion's scathing wrath they all knew.

"Come on, out with it!" Albion barked. He was this morning quite ready to go on the offensive first, feeling better than he had in months.

The cagey crowd still wouldn't bite and remained silent.

"Surely there must be one of you brilliant sleuths that have formulated a better idea. Step forward now!" Albion barked.

Still no takers as the room remained silent.

Finally, one raised her hand as he knew she would.

"Are you saying we're looking for two Jacks?" she timidly asked standing half way up, not willing to commit her whole body for derisive exposure.

"Either two clever human murderers or one human murderer and one demon, or two demons, take your pick!" Albion sneered directly at her; the thin, lithe figured officer Iris Muldoon; his usual scapegoat, causing her to rapidly retreat downward.

Snickers now erupted in the room.

"Funny is it? You all think it's funny? Whatever is happening all we have is a bunch of dead folks whose numbers are growing and still no suspects! Not a lead from any of you! What's funny about that?" Albion snarled.

"If at least one is a demon, well, how do we catch them? And what exactly is a demon?" the brave female asked anew from her now sitting position; her momentarily safe hiding place.

"Finally, a good question," Albion remarked, "I don't know what a demon is, but the dictionary defines one as an evil spirit originating in hell. Other than that you'd have to consult your priests since I don't have any experience except in the apprehension of the human types."

"And, how do we catch it?" she repeated timidly.

Albion shrugged and said nothing, but after a bit of time to rattle them he dismissed them with a wave of his arm. The loud silence of the all too obvious unanswered question still hung heavily around Albion's shoulders in the room long after they had gone.

~~~~~

Dave couldn't believe his luck, since he'd never had any of the good type before as best he could remember. He pinched himself again to be sure. They'd hung out all the early evening and now the very late evening found them in one of London's livelier night spots; The King's Crown. The place was restaurant, pub, pool hall, and dance hall combined and it was jumping.

Heda proved to be a very amiable and likeable comrade and a good dancer to boot.

The slick, multi-colored lighted from below dance floor served them well this evening as a way to get acquainted better. Dave learned a bit about her life and aspirations as the evening progressed and she learned a good bit about him too.

Finally, after dinner, and quite sloshed and thus getting up his false beer courage Dave asked a question that normally being sober; he'd have the good sense to avoid.

"You're a Moslem and you drink?" Dave asked rudely while in his cups much farther than he'd been in a long time.

"Sure, I'm just like most Moslems and Christians. I pick and choose which rules I want to follow," she answered with no animosity, she being quite used to that by now usual question.

Dave was now truly becoming amazed at the average Britons' propensity to drink and tolerate large quantities of warm beer along with a lot of whiskey and still be able to talk, walk, and dance without falling out.

They were feeling a bit tipsy and finally decided to sit and chat a while in the dark, dimly lit joint. At this moment Dave impulsively severed his com link with Cresasern for his own privacy issues and hopes.

"Gin and tonics for us both," Dave told the waitress as Heda fell into the oval shaped booth beside him and caught her breath, laughing. She had to admit; she was having a good time in spite of herself.

"Doubles?" she asked tipsily.

"Of course," Dave answered, feeling higher than he had been in a long time.

Once served, they began gingerly sipping their drinks when Dave suddenly noticed the two burly men standing over them rudely blocking out the dancers on the floor.

Dave and Heda looked up at the two imposing, blue suited figures and they wondered what was up now.

The two somber interlopers were tall, stocky and ruddy faced and neither appeared to be smiling in the least. In fact their sneers seemed sewn on Dave noticed with his drink induced blurred faculties.

"Inspector Albion wants to see you down at the station!" the bigger one shouted loudly, above the din in the room.

"Not tonight, I got a date," Dave slurred back defiantly.

"Tonight---! Now---!" shouted the other one, who suddenly grabbed Dave roughly by the arm and yanked him up and right out of the booth as though he was a rag doll.

Heda shouted, "Let's see some I.D.!"

Number two blatantly opened his jacket to reveal an awfully large automatic laser pistol tucked into his belt and snarled, "Is this good enough?"

Heda rose and said defiantly, "You can't do this!"

"Watch us sister!" gruffly said number one who suddenly grabbed Heda up also and soon Dave and Heda found themselves being unceremoniously manhandled first through the throng of dancers and then past the busy bar on their way out of the club by strong hands.

Heda and her captor led the way through the throng of gyrating drunks and soon exiting the club the four of them stepped out into the foggy street and felt the sting of the cold night air hitting them in the faces as Big Ben ominously tolled two somewhere off in the distance.

~~~~~

Morgan scratched his crotch and yawned discretely as he listened halfhearted to the acolyte's confession.

This part he hated the most. Listening to the same mindless drivel day in and day out had long since crossed his eyes with consternation and vexation. The lad today was crying as usual about having prurient thoughts about another male acolyte. What could you expect; locking up three dozen men in a cloister with nothing interesting to do, of course some will snap, of course some of them are freaks, Morgan reasoned.

"Oh for something new and interesting from these dolts," Morgan groaned to himself. "A murder, or an armed robbery, or how about an embezzlement, that would be nice," he laughed to himself, feeling his bile rising in disgust.

As his anger and jealousy rose against the lad who at least felt something sexual; something that Morgan hadn't felt in the least in over twenty years, Morgan fumed. For a split second Morgan thought hard on busting through the thin, wooden partition separating him from the young, stupid boy and grabbing the lad roughly in both his hands and strangling him slowly to death.

Luckily that impulse passed quickly as Morgan was having a tougher time lately controlling his baser urges. Thank GOD for the Ministry Of Information giving him some needed release in that area, he thought.

"Say three hail Mary's and take a cold shower as soon as possible," Morgan snidely advised the lad.

"You think that'll work?" the lad asked innocently, naively, stupidly.

"Works for me!" Morgan cruelly answered, exiting the confessional with much haste stifling a guffaw, and as his bile rose anew; he headed for the head ahead of an accident, he hoped.

Later, sheepishly glancing sideways at his, he thought, good left side in the men's room mirror, Morgan wiped his sweaty, clammy, face and he remembered: Bright Gate, the idea, had been hatched one evening between Morgan and his two, fairly unknown at the time, other drinking buddies; Edgar Blight and Alistair Morris, now referred to by Morgan only as number one and number two.

Over their warm mead they conceived the idea to take over the old, decrepit, abandoned, run down "Abbey of Tears" here outside the rustic hamlet of Harpenden and convert it into a cloister and a detox center for the rich. Edgar they nominated for the position of head friar because he knew the scriptures better than the other two.

To their amazement the idea actually took off and now the three were extremely rich men. Now the place housed the aforementioned 36 faux monkish acolytes as a front and to provide cheap labor and now on staff they boasted three psychiatrists and psychologists, and enough professional staff to handle the throng of rich burned out men and women sorely in need of a clean out.

Now they picked and chose amongst the rich gentry for the very richest to bleed dry in more ways than one. Morgan and numbers one and two now had squirreled away millions of £ pounds between them in Britain and Zurich, all that from one drunken night, what a laugh, he thought.

No, now Morgan readily admitted to himself that he didn't work for the Ministry of Information for the money; no, he did it for the sheer love of the activity of killing. And that was what was upsetting his stomach and severely bothering Morgan this day; the Ministry had been strangely silent these past four days since the Claypool murder and Morgan feared that his one legal pleasurable outlet might be running dry and so he sweated anew, fretting his danger laden options of going it alone once again.

~~~~~

"They're not real coppers! Run!" Heda loudly whispered to the stupefied Dave as they were being led to a large dark car parked up the street away from the front of the bar.

"What---?" Dave asked drunkenly.

"Run you fool!" Heda shouted swiftly kicking her captor in his groin, thus she slipped her attacker's grasp and headed away up into the fog shrouded street momentarily disappearing from view, loudly running in her heels for all she was worth.

Finally getting the gist of what was really happening through his ossified brain Dave drunkenly swung at his captor and surprisingly punched his fellow in the nose a good, solid blow, and then free, he followed as best as his drunken feet could follow heading up the gray clouded street behind Heda's footfalls.

"This way!" she shouted ahead as she abruptly cut hard left up into an alley.

Dave dumbly followed hearing the swearing men loudly following closely behind.

Suddenly Dave ran right up into Heda's back who had stopped in her tracks for some reason that Dave wasn't yet privy to. They both almost fell onto the cobblestone street momentarily, but quick natural reflexes barely overcame inebriation and saved them as they drunkenly swayed holding each other for support.

"That wall wasn't here before, I'm sure," she said sadly referring to the all too obvious large wooden structure now obtusely blocking the back of the alley that now stopped their forward progress toward an escape.

Dave now began to sober up as he regarded the tall wooden wall and then heard the two angry men close on them and enter the alley behind them.

"We got him now. The girl's with him too. What's the order?" asked the bigger one into his ear phone piece all the while swabbing his nose's bleeding red spigot.

Dave and Heda barely heard the reply but it was, "gas them, leave the girl there, unharmed you hear, and bring the man!"

With that the two so-called policemen pulled out their long black gas sticks and pointed them right at the two frightened hapless people caught like rats in a trap at the end of the alley.

The growing gray fog seemed to conspire against Dave and Heda also as it too swirled anew behind the advancing thugs and illuminated their immense bulks, both eerily, sending a new fright into the hapless, trapped duo.

Dave, though scared, bravely stepped forward, pushing Heda back, and with both fists raised in a fighter's stance albeit a drunken one, he hoped somehow to protect her.

Heda thought it a gallant but foolish gesture and she tensed also for a fight.

"Here suckers!" happily shouted "bleeding spigot." as the two thugs now activated their gas sticks pointing at Dave and Heda.

The gas sticks popped, chugged, and spewed out a thick, green gaseous concoction that hit Dave first and then Heda head on quickly and it dropped them both like a ton of bricks where they stood immediately, Dave falling first.

As the ground came up to hit Dave's head with a hard, loud, thud he thought that he heard a commotion begin suddenly in the alley.

When Heda fell heavily onto his chest his eyes opened momentarily and he saw above, flashing lights, fast swirling shadows and then the last thing he heard and saw as he succumbed to a deep forceful sleep was sudden, loudly sparkling gunfire.

Then reverberated in the alley much more loud and frightening gunfire, rushing winds, and then even more echoes of curses and gunfire from the two men that attacked him and Heda and he knew, with his eyes shut, without a shadow of a doubt that they wouldn't ever be waking up from this night's mayhem at all!

Chapter 7

Sunday, October 16, 2016

Albion sat back uncomfortably in the hard stiff backed chair and felt his hot anger rising, rising by the minute as he regarded the three old men facing him safely from behind their tall, imposing podium; denying him probably.

The last time for him in this same hot seat had been with the full six wigged old dignitaries present. The fact that today there were but three attending, portended doom for sure, he surmised with his calculating mind now mathematically crunching the odds against him.

For one thing; this time they once again never deigned to summon him given the severity of the crisis; he had to beg for an audience despite the loud hue and cry from the populace, and Parliament, and even his own flustered superiors in New Scotland Yard.

These three old men soared above all that; the people, big and small, and the government, and Albion suspected; even the King.

"We have--- seriously considered--- your request," began Sir Archibald Sleetel, the oldest, and certainly the fattest, senior head official in the Ministry of Information, down from his middle seat, high behind the mahogany podium before Albion.

Albion inwardly fought to control the rise of his blood pressure and anger as he waited for the inevitable.

"We can't see our way clear to allow that heinous device to be used again. Why compound our one error with another? We're sorry," chimed in Sir Isaac Roland, the tall, thin, and distinguished looking junior member of the triumvirate sitting to Sir Sleetel's left with no obvious genuine concern for the people's welfare shown.

Sir Reginald Bowden simply sat silently in his floating chair avidly, though seemingly detached, watching the proceedings.

"You do realize it's only for the public's safety?" Albion asked, pleadingly.

"We determine what is in the public's safety and best interests!" commanded Sir Roland with a loud rap of his well worn gavel.

"What---happened to those old tried and true police methods, you---know; gather evidence, interview witnesses, form a---profile,---whatever?" Sir Sleetel asked in his own unique often publicly derided, semi-retarded, slurred fashion.

"Whoever or whatever it is doing this is they don't leave the usual tracks. Either it's a world-class professional, or a supernatural demon is suspected," Albion said seriously.

"Demon---? Posh! See, that's what wrong with your investigation; you're off the track. You need to be more objective, far saner, less inclined to fantasy, mysticism, and defeatism. Get cracking with the tried and true police methods and you'll see results!" preached Sir Ronald, clucking and shaking his index finger paternally at Albion.

"Whatever. The---use of the device is---denied. You're---excused!" barked Sir Sleetel scratching his old powdered wig absent-mindedly.

Albion then cleared his throat and bravely asked, "Well, harrumph----can I at least have the disc from the Berner Street incident? That way I'll at least know something?"

The three once again conferred animatedly.

"No!" tersely shouted Sir Roland finally.

"Why?" Albion bravely asked as he rose.

"Have a care Inspector! There are forces at work here that could prove to be most dangerous to you! National security is at stake!" Sir Reginald Bowden barked ominously, breaking his long silence and fixing Albion with an evil cold stare that iced Albion's veins instantly.

Albion exited the Ministry building with his anger growing and his old copper's suspicions fully aroused. He stopped on the steps and tapped down a pinch of non-toxic tobacco into his ivory bull's head pipe and thought. He thought of how quickly those three in there had approved the BBC's initial Extraminator "catch" on Berner Street because, he figured, it had served their purposes at the time to start and mask this thing. He thought that now they disallowed his presently requested "catch" because not only would it not serve their purposes, it would reveal the truth about who really attacked the crowd that night.

Albion reckoned now with a degree of certainty of at least 78% that he had just left the presence of the cabal behind the ripper killings or if they were not involved directly, they certainly knew more about the killings than he did.

One thing the three inside didn't know was that the shard of silver metal found at Trinny Simpson's murder was traced back by Professor Billingsly to a watcher buzzer drone belonging to this very same Ministry of Information, Albion laughed.

This day still was not a total loss, he surmised, but most enlightening. His anger now returned along with his long dormant mental powers and he was surprised to notice at that moment that his long dormant libido was beginning to prosper also. He would have to try that one out on Florence tonight, he reckoned happily.

~~~~~

Dave awoke with a start of confusion as to where he was and with a hot burning sensation suddenly erupting on his chest. Rising, he regarded with much disdain the clumsy service robot happily spilling hot coffee on him. For a split second Dave considered slapping the dumb, blocky shaped machine slap happy.

"Sorry about that," Heda apologized, lithely sweeping into her living room and approaching the sofa containing the half rising, but still sleepy Dave and to the side; his mechanical antagonist. She sheepishly grabbed the hot coffee out of the grasp of her tin helper and offered it up to Dave herself.

She was modestly clothed in a pink, fluffy, terry cloth robe and she was toweling her long wet hair most fetchingly Dave noticed as he gained some semblance of normal consciousness.

"Thanks," Dave said slowly sipping the hot brew as the robot, somehow aware of Dave's mean intentions toward it, retreated backwards into the safety of the kitchen.

Heda sat down on the sofa at Dave's feet and with shining brown eyes regarded him a long time with a most quizzical, odd, staring regard.

"I know, I think it's strange too," Dave said, avoiding her stare.

"The loo is over there. You really need a shower!" she offered, frowning her nose up most intensely.

Looking at his haggard face in her bathroom mirror explained what she meant. Down the entire left side of his face and splattered about his shirt and pants was a fine spray of dried bright red blood. Shock once again visited him as he regarded proof positive that last night was by no means but a bad dream.

Wasting no time he jumped into her hot shower and planned a quick trip downtown to buy more clothes on the way back to his hotel immediately. Once washed, he rejoined her in the living room.

"You sure know how to show a girl a good time," she jibed sarcastically, "though hanging around you is decidedly exciting in a most dangerous fashion."

Dave nodded between more hot sips of the dark, sobering, life renewing brew.

"Thanks again," Heda said seriously, with both of them understanding her unspoken, deeper, meaning.

Last night, it had been Dave who awoke first in the darkened alley.

He awoke slowly and happily realizing that he wasn't dead, or shot, slowly rose from under Heda's body and took in a most harrowing sight.

The two goons were bloodily laid out on their backs in the alley with their guns still grasped in their dead hands right close to them. One lay against the wooden wall while the other rested over against the far brick wall. Both appeared to have been butchered in a most savage, and callous, fashion as evidenced by their harrowingly bloody remains left exhibited out in such a blatant display. Dave nervously wondered by whom!

Dave at once felt utter sickness cloud over his fast fleeting drunkenness as he slowly took in the cold, frightening, horror of the sight before him. He noted that the bloody alley walls were all pockmarked with many random laser and bullet holes, obviously from the two deceased men's still smoking, warm weapons.

"What in the hell happened here?" he frighteningly wondered aloud. The thought of the Ripper or as the papers now stated: "Rippers" plural, obviously came to Dave's fuzzy mind and he wondered why hadn't the fiend killed him and Heda too?

Dave now somehow gathered his lately missing wits and suppressed his growing fear induced trepidation and intelligently, quickly, scanned the past around and in the alley with his implanted device. Noting his eye screen's time counter as 2:15 A.M.; he knew how far back to go. Once that two second task was done he downloaded the signal back to Cresasern over an open Wi-Fi channel.

As Heda roused, Dave attempted to shield her from the morbid bloody display so close by to them by grabbing and holding her close, vainly directing her eyes away from the grisly sight.

Her throbbing sobs as she held onto him led Dave to believe he wasn't entirely successful in his attempt.

Holding her close he felt her supple body and pert breasts rocking against him and Dave oddly, inadvertently, and humorously, so out of place as to be ludicrous, thought his new found spate of good luck was still holding.

"We got to get out of here!" Dave implored as he slowly helped her rise, "can you walk?"

"I'll try," was all she whimpered, as Dave held her up and led her out of the alley, both weaving precariously.

Somehow they shakily escaped the dark, smelly abattoir of an alley as a few passersby began to discover that something awful had occurred there. Then they passed through and left the small crowd now converging on the alley and made their way out into the foggy night without too much hassle.

Soon the shrill sound of the night bobby's whistle loudly, far behind them, only served to hasten their escape.

A sky cab took them to Heda's top floor penthouse Greenwich borough flat, with the talkative Jamaican pilot proving to be an absolute total nuisance all the way. The quick flight zooming high over the darkened rooftops of London only served to cause the two to huddle closer together as the ground sped by below fast, too fast this night for his still queasy stomach, Dave noted trying not to get sick.

Reaching their destination; she wouldn't take no for an answer and so he went up with her. Actually she didn't want to be alone this harrowing night in spite of the social hazards possible from their all too brief history and of course, the drugging they had both been subject to.

Once safely in her apartment, Dave shucked her heels for her and tucked her into her bed while still clothed, comfortably under the covers. Resisting hard two very improper impulses, he left her alone and closing her door looked for his sleeping place this night on the living room couch as her home service robot simply watched him suspiciously with its blood red eyes all a nosily twinkling.

Dave was too tired to take much notice of the vigilant robot and he fell hard back onto the couch and sought sleep immediately.

Before dozing off Dave's ear piece crackled with Cresasern's loudly booming baritone voice, "Don't replay that last transmission. I'll see you tomorrow downtown. We have to talk. I repeat, under no circumstances replay that image!"

"Breakfast is served!" suddenly interrupted the red eyed robot in a whiny, tinny voice.

The interruption brought Dave back to the present and soon he and Heda sat across from each other at her small kitchen table eating a quiet somber breakfast as many seriously troubled thoughts wafted amongst them.

Dave for his part was quite embarrassed and unsure of how to proceed with Heda, as if proceeding was a feasible option, her being a Moslem and all.

Heda wondered fearfully if it was wise to invest herself emotionally in someone who obviously had so little time left to live if the past was any indicator of the future that is.

With those unseen, dark storm clouds forming over them they ate quietly while the red eyed robot beamed due to its first apparently successful preparation of a breakfast.

~~~~~

Dr. Harry Griscom was busier now than he'd been in years. As he busied himself over the two newest cadavers in his charge he wondered why the police department continued to scrimp on hiring new staff despite his numerous entreaties.

Albion keenly watched the good doctor expertly saw this, invade that, and coolly weigh whatever he removed with a growing respect. The man moved like a practiced machine, deftly doing this and that with little wasted motion, with smooth, very smooth movements much like a dancer dancing a dance of death, Albion waxed poetically.

Albion gave Griscom his patented cross-eyed look of; "what's up?"

Griscom shucked his gloves and began to wash his hands at the sink making it a point to ignore Albion.

Albion played.

He began to whistle a ditty he knew vexed the doctor. The ditty; Scotland Forever poorly escaped his pursed lips and Albion happily saw Griscom visibly wince, and then wince again and he knew he had him.

"I'd say the same fellow that hacked up Vince Sewell did these two also," Griscom finally said.

"Not the others?" Albion asked, almost gleefully as the doctor confirmed his lurking suspicions.

"No not the others! These cuts here are made with a much different, a much longer blade and in a different pattern. I'd stake my life on it!" Griscom cried.

Albion could barely contain his inner satisfaction.

"Looks like you actually do have two different perpetrators!" Griscom continued. "Besides the notes sent in to the Evening Standard matches exactly those sent back in 1888, while the ones sent to you doesn't match near as well."

Albion now gave the doctor his always expected questioning look of: "demon?" by holding up two fingers behind his own head.

Griscom shook his shaggy head in the negative, as usual in that regard.

A young, flustered cop came in with a paper which he gingerly handed to Albion while obviously averting his eyes from the two large butchered cadavers laying quietly over on their cold steel slabs.

Albion read the note as the young cop ran out of the room as fast as he could and smiled his Cheshire cat smile which infuriated Griscom anew.

Now it was Griscom's turn; as his own "what's up?" look was etched across his usually somber face to the chagrin of Albion.

"It took quite a bit of digging through classified and hidden information, but their prints finally came up and Andrew Vansler, and Fred L. Beasley here are your new unwilling tenants, both of them show up as "independent contractors" for the Ministry of Information," Albion positively beamed, pointing to the two cold, prone fellows.

"By the way, I've been meaning to give you this for an age," Dr. Griscom said happily handing over a small sheet of metallic paper.

"What is it?" Albion asked taking it in his hand.

"It's the identity of the 1888 Ripper, the Ministry of Information's forensics department matched his mug to photos provided back then," Dr. Griscom said. "Can you believe who it is?"

"I'm not surprised," Albion stated after glancing at the holo-picture and august name noted below. This tiny metallic paper would now serve as an individual memory item in the police data bank; wherever it was placed its contents could be retrieved instantly, thus no more lost documents ever.

Albion snickered to think that this bit of late information, some 128 years old was all the Ministry wanted him to have.

"Some things never change," Albion stated smiling gleefully.

Dr. Griscom wisely didn't share Albion's glee and frowned; he knew that this case was fast becoming one kettle of old, dirty fish that once overturned, could smell them all up before it was righted and closed up again.

~~~~~

The small, spartanly furnished round room was barely lit by the single candle burning by the bed stand. The weak light poorly illuminated the room's single occupant; the man kneeling in the middle of the floor, rocking violently, as he prayed.

For prayers were certainly needed this morning, Morgan wailed plaintively in his troubled mind.

The urge to kill had came up on him again most fiercely earlier this morning in such a violent rush that overwhelmed him and thrust him unto insanity's very open door. For over a week he'd waited in vain for the call from Clive, the call that looked like it never would come again now.

That cold, hard, reality forced Morgan to plot on taking the train up to Leeds for some kidney pie, an Aire riverfront stroll, and hopefully a personal kill. A kill that included strangulation figured most prominently in his sick wishes, for that was what he most desired now.

"That would do quite nicely," he quipped insanely to himself.

To strangle someone up close with his strong hard hands and feel their life leave their struggling bodies was what he most craved now unto blind desire, besides, to use his knife was verboten by the Ministry except when they instructed.

That same burning blind desire now forced him down the round turreted stairway down into the cloister's dark, dank, basement around three this morning seeking some succor. It wouldn't do to kill someone on the cloister grounds, for obvious reasons, though he knew a few he'd like to do anyway whatever the risk, he madly reasoned.

The wet, smelly basement happily yielded up a few rats that he proceeded to easily catch and butcher in order to sate his unnatural lust.

His partly sane mind cried out to him that he had surely hit rock bottom now. He was on the third rat when he became violently sick at what he was doing. He violently retched, and somehow he soon found himself climbing on his hands and knees back up the ancient stone steps one step at a time, while he imagined that the imbedded gargoyles in the walls berated him, and mocked him, all the while feeling that he was really climbing up out of something more than just the abbey's hellish cellar in more ways than one.

Reaching his room he fell to his knees and prayed for all he was worth and soon the unexpected happened; his blood lust suddenly ebbed out of him in an overwhelming wash of exhilaration and heretofore unfelt pleasure as he felt a healthy stirring below in his loins that he hadn't felt even a glimmer of in over twenty five years.

Morgan fell suddenly spread wide armed, and prostrate himself down on the hard, cold brick floor, crushing an insect below him with an oddly loud crackle, he sobbed hard, sobbed the first happy sobs of the coming salvation that he was sure of was his.

~~~~~

Monday, October 16, 2016

Dave admired the beautifully awe inspiring, heady view from up here on the thirtieth floor of the Wilshire Building sitting smack dab amid its similar brothers in the middle of Westminster City, the shining centerpiece of London's 32 sprawling boroughs.

They were in the glassed tower Cresasern Corporate headquarters. The vast expanse of London lay in glittering spires below stretching seemingly forever. The sky above the city was uncharacteristically; a clear cloudless clean light blue thus a sky cab or two could be seen hovering in the distance quite easily. On such a beautiful day Dave just couldn't imagine that any bad things might lay ahead for him.

"I can see you followed my orders," Cresasern said giving Dave the Evening Standard paper.

"Of course I did, besides I've been busy," Dave absent mindedly answered, missing an opportunity to ask how Cresasern knew he hadn't looked, taking the paper and reading the article Cresasern had underlined under the title: "Police Stumped Again as Jack Strikes Once More!".

"That article aptly describes what little they know about what happened in that alley last night," Cresasern quipped while forlornly looking out the west side full wall of the glass surrounding his office, his large arms folded behind him.

"They don't even know who those two dead men were?" Dave answered, surprised.

"I'll bet Albion does, like me," Cresasern said abruptly.

"You do?" Dave asked quite surprised.

"That was a truly bone headed maneuver you made by turning off your communications link!" Cresasern suddenly barked, his light brown eyes flashing genuine anger.

"I'm gonna do better boss!" Dave shouted back angrily, sarcastically.

"I wish you wouldn't use that term "gonna". It's the prime action verb of the backsliding, shiftless, good for nothing loser! Its use always denotes a lie to the one it's directed to and besides, doesn't fool the "unstupid" folks of the world it's used on one bit!" Cresasern shouted.

Dave, feeling unjustly berated began to feel his own anger rise anew and he wondered why Cresasern was treating him like a child.

Cresasern now walked about and began breathing evenly; thus he brought his temper under control as Dave retreated deeper into the article, quite happy not to see any mention to him and Heda specifically. The article did say that the police were avidly seeking a young couple; description fuzzy, for questioning in the matter though.

"I've seen the hand of GOD in my life many times. Have you?" Cresasern asked calmly, unexpectedly.

"Can't say as I have. Why?" Dave answered as his anger and resentment began to grow even stronger.

"Perhaps it's because you haven't looked hard enough? Perhaps you should try again? Perhaps after today you will?" Cresasern asked knowingly, his cryptic, superior attitude was starting to definitely vex Dave.

As usual, the rich folks who grew up within a two parent household could always preach about such matters, Dave knowingly groused inwardly. Of course those rich types who had their prayers answered for some specific bauble or toy would say what Cresasern said. Those who prayed for the very basics in life without any discernible success like him, Dave, though, possessed a completely different, negative take on the subject.

"I want you to see something, bear in mind you probably won't understand it!" Cresasern warned, pulling out a remote and activating his overhead projector.

Suddenly the expensively furnished posh high rise office was bathed in the red, blue, yellow, and greenish light of an Extraminator replay. At once Dave and Cresasern were surrounded by holographic visions depicting past events in the dark deadly alley. The images; in vividly colored three dimensions abruptly appeared around, amongst, and surrounding Cresasern and Dave and shockingly showed them what all happened there last night.

Dave painfully watched as the two goons gassed him and Heda. Then something strange appeared. That something; it was large, way over twenty feet tall, gray, and fuzzy appearing in its inverted pyramid shape as it swirled in moving inhumanly fast; it sped into the scene and attacked the two goons. What it was, Dave couldn't tell; it was but a blur to him.

The whirling tornado shaped blur proceeded to attack viciously and then raise the goons high off the ground enfolding them in its rapidly swirling vortex high above the prone bodies of Heda and him, and as it shredded the goons, they seemed to shout and shoot about wildly all over to no avail.

The two struggling victims tossed wildly this way and that as long, vicious cuts appeared on their bodies in a most surreally frightening manner. The whirling gray blur, once done its grisly work of shredding them, cast them haphazardly about the alley and it then swirled away out of the alley immediately.

Dave was utterly flabbergasted at what he had just beheld and vainly strived mentally, logically, to somehow understand it on some basic level of human understanding. The visible proof of why the bloody red spray had appeared on him and Heda came painfully to mind as he watched, and he blessed his stars that they both had been unconscious during the time the entire ordeal was happening so close above them to those two unfortunate fellows.

"Can you slow the replay down so we can see what that thing was?" Dave avidly urged with his agitation quite apparently growing.

"We have, and it's still no different. At first we thought you'd mistakenly, drunkenly, recorded in fast forward motion or something, but that wasn't the case," Cresasern said sadly.

Dave sat down hard in the chair and felt at once fearful, shook up all the way down to his feet, totally lost as a shot of cold fear went straight up his spine.

"What was it?" was all that Dave could muster.

"A demon! A real demon from hell I fear," Cresasern cried with an air of utter despair.

"That's why I knew you hadn't seen the replay. It's something to really shake your soul up! Huh---?" Cresasern said ominously.

Want to see it again?" Cresasern then asked.

"Hell no!" Dave shouted.

Chapter 8

Wednesday, October 19, 2016

Passersby in the halls outside Sir Reginald Bowden's fifth floor opulent office quarters in the Ministry of Information building, if they stopped this morning and put their ear to his massive door, as many often have; they would hear the usual racket. Loud shouts, crashes, banging of all sorts, the usual ruckus they would imagine, but they would be wrong this day. This day instead of Sir Reginald making the most obtuse noises it was his familiar Clive Waddell ranting and raving to the rafters.

"I tell you its Morgan who's doing this! We have to do something! He should be killed! Fast---!" Clive frantically railed as he paced nervously back and forth with his much over agitated arm motions flailing wildly about.

Sir Reginald floated, swaying silently, while he coolly regarded the mad young man in his lair with a twinge of humor.

He knew for a fact that it wasn't Morgan doing it. A myriad bevy of his spy buzzers disguised as birds, and bats ringed Bright Gate now, and had been doing so for as long as he had employed Morgan. Couple them with the numerous fake arachnids, cockroaches, beetles, and flies; all spying on Morgan gave Sir Reginald the peace of mind regarding Morgan's innocence that he always needed when dealing with men of this ilk. In fact Sir Reginald was acutely aware of how much Morgan now vigorously, chafed painfully due to the lack of his murderous needs being satisfied.

Of course, Sir Reginald wasn't about to tell Clive any of this. "No, that doesn't serve my purpose at all," he thought. Besides Clive might figure correctly that I have him also infested with such similar bugs, Sir Reginald noted wryly.

Still, Sir Reginald was concerned, very concerned most definitely, but long ago when he still walked on his own legs he knew the wisdom of never letting them know you were sweating--- never!

"You may be right," Sir Reginald said flatly.

"Maybe---?" Clive ranted nervously. "After what happened to Andy and Fred, it'll probably be me next---!"

"Stop pacing! I have an idea," Sir Reginald ordered blithely, too blithely to sooth Clive's growing out of control concern.

"I can't!" Clive shouted stridently.

Sir Reginald suddenly swooped from behind his desk and swiftly rammed into Clive hard with his floating chair knocking the agitated fellow first to the ground and then pushed him against the far wall, finally stopping, thus pinning Clive's left leg under the hovering vehicle.

"Blimey! You've broke my bloody blooming leg! What's wrong with you?" Clive cried painfully, unwittingly revealing his heretofore well hidden Cockney lower class heritage, trying futilely to extricate his pinned left leg.

"It's not broke. Give a listen you dolt! I want you to take this Extraminator thing back to that alley and record what happened there last night. It's set to do its job, all you have to do is wave it about after you press this here red button! No brain strain needed! Got that?" Sir Reginald shouted easing back his chair and freeing Clive who gingerly took the smallish camcorder device offered up in Sir Reginald's one good hand.

Clive limped up, and sat hard in the fat chair in front of the desk and regarded the device intently while rubbing his surely bruised sore left leg.

"Here's something no gentleman should be without also. It'll help you walk with your new limp and if Morgan is the one you seek, well it'll help you with him too!" Sir Reginald laughed as he tossed Clive a black onyx walking stick tipped with a gold handle.

Clive caught the stick in mid air and grasping its handle pulled on it back hard to reveal the two foot and a half long sharp straight steel rapier blade hidden within its sheath. This caused a wide grin to appear on his heretofore troubled face from ear to ear.

"Are you still taking that I.G.F. insulin growth factor?" Sir Reginald asked.

"Yes sir!" Clive answered, happily regarding his new toys with much childish awe.

"Well, have your doctor double your dose, you might need it!" Sir Reginald barked, summarily dismissing his charge with a wave.

Watching the young, miscreant leave brought a twinge of a tear of regret to Sir Reginald's tired seventy two year old eyes. The young fellow just couldn't help himself; blood will out, sadly reasoned Sir Reginald. Clive came from a long line of smugglers, cut purses, and murderous thieves, it was in his blood. His father died in Newgate Prison serving life for burglary and murder. If only Clive's stunted, clouded mind could see past his inbred criminal genes, well, the man could have enjoyed a successful straight career as a model or actor; he sported the requisite "media approved" Nordic looks that they were looking for.

Sir Reginald now deeply regretted choosing this one over some of the other more promising applicants, more and more as time went on.

"And so did I once!" Sir Reginald suddenly shouted, "I was young, strong, and handsome until Leila crippled me," he murmured under his breath.

His mind's eye now returned to that fateful day; with the beautiful but spoiled Leila driving and jabbering drunkenly all too fast. She missed her turn while berating him, for what he didn't remember now, and hit a tree and rolled the Aston car. Luckily for her she died quickly, for Sir Reginald mused, he would have killed her slowly for what she had done to him. Now he simply contented himself with the title of Britain's Misogynist King, and for good reason, he laughed.

~~~~~

Dave pushed in the red wooden double doors to the Cock and Bull pub roughly, bravely, like he owned the place. It was the first pub to be encountered around the corner from Cresasern's office and Dave couldn't wait. Bellying up to the bar he ordered a double Scotch whiskey from the totally surprised, gray haired ruddy faced bartender. It didn't escape Dave's notice that the locals all immediately stopped their private conversations to openly gawk at him. They appeared to be mostly all aged over sixty; pensioners to a fault, Dave suspected.

How people could spend their entire lives working for years on end just to end up on a bright sunny day hiding in a dark bar escaped his reasoning. Were they watching him because he was the only black in the bar or was it his youth? Dave didn't know and right now he didn't care.

Overhead, the Holo-TV blared out: "Space station Alpha-2 goes quiet after opening canister containing spores from Enceladus!.....Large white fur covered ape discovered in Himalayas!.....Russia easily crushes Moslem insurrection in southeastern provinces!.....Crude oil falls to ten £ pounds a barrel!....Feline flu breaks out again in Florida!"

Ignoring the news and the pub crawlers Dave ordered another double and quaffed that down as fast as possible, and then he left the dark bar feeling a bit tipsy, seeking the bright sunlight once again.

Traveling past Piccadilly he soon, finally found the entrance to the tree lined Hyde Park and therein a stone bench, which he took warmly to immediately despite its hard seat. Sitting out here under the Sun's healing rays he once again began to think rationally. His first impulse was to catch the first flight out back to the U.S.

What Cresasern had showed him earlier, the other day, had frightened him more than anything else ever in his life, and deep in his soul he knew that he couldn't and most likely wouldn't survive another encounter with that whatever it was thing that was killing people at its whim in this town.

His second thought was even worse; where could you run to escape something like that? The answer; nowhere! And why didn't it kill him and Heda? It certainly had the time, if not the inclination.

He could hear Cresasern saying, "We can't shirk our Christian mandate to fight evil, human or supernatural, or we're helping; joining that evil!"

How do you fight something that can squash you so easily? Vulnerable and marked for death, doomed, that's us, that's about it, he thought despondently.

Reaching inside behind his new clean shirt collar he grasped his small golden crucifix and held hard on to it for dear life and sadly contemplated his boss's latest orders, as the crucifix thankfully, but unexpectedly warmed him from head to toe.

This was turning out to be the strangest job he'd ever had. Tomorrow morning he had an appointment in the "lion's den" as Cresasern referred to it, and he was everything but happy about it, but his assigned task today was not going to be an easy one either.

Dave felt the hard concrete bench below him grow colder, and he painfully remembered his own beginnings as Cresasern had described them. The symbolism of this and that other similar park bench in Philadelphia long ago now began to disturb him, so gathering up his courage Dave then hailed a land cab and upon entering said simply to the cabbie, "take me to New Scotland Yard."

~~~~~

"It's exciting to discover a new piece to the puzzle of our physical and metaphysical existence. Of course some of those new pieces may prove to quite disconcerting and distasteful!" Cresasern said this more to himself than to his guest.

"Its funny how little the average man knows concerning his everyday environment." Cresasern continued.

"Most people don't know that the surface rotational speed of the Earth at its equator is a thousand miles per hour. Couple that with this planet spinning around the Sun yearly, couple that with the Sun carrying us around on its own journey, couple that with the Milky Way carrying us around as it makes its own orbit. Couple that with this universe dragging us along wherever on its own unknown expanding journey and what you have is this room, this city, this entire planet traveling at speeds exceeding half a million miles per hour with none of us people literally stuck here, feeling the motion at all and thus none the wiser! Physicists may call it earth space time mechanics; I call it GOD's divine balancing act!" Cresasern preached avidly.

The guest didn't respond, having heard all this heady postulation many times before. Listening outside in the next room during the entire interview, including Cresasern's last speech, with the suddenly melancholy Dave Asher, the guest now suffered through it all once again.

The guest had to admit that Cresasern knew his stuff, and hoped, but hadn't usually found it the case, that the few listeners fortunate enough to hear him possessed the requisite apparatus betwixt their ears to understand and profit from him. The guest simply, tentatively, humorously, pressed his right foot down to the floor trying to see if he felt any untoward motion of the earth.

Benjamin Cresasern wearily watched the replay once again, for the tenth time, he reckoned tiredly.

The more he watched, the harder it was to watch the same butchering of men over and over again, but watch it he must, he knew. He watched mainly because he had seen something odd in the replay and his highly paid scientific staff had confirmed it also.

The odd thing was that the whirling, blurred murdering cloud had actually moved toward the two prone bodies of Dave and Heda at the same time that it had moved on and grabbed up the two goons.

The anomaly was almost imperceptible at first, but now after watching it so often it became quite obvious to Cresasern that something unseen had actually deterred the powerful unholy beast from also grabbing up the two prone helpless people.

"You know that I long ago believed, and the Extraminator has recently proven, that all mankind are cousins, no matter what we look like on the outside. No matter what those ignorant good ole boys preach, we're the same inside to the violent chagrin of many. We all came from the same people out of Africa long ago. I also believe that since we all were made in GOD's image we are as a species, evolving into the next level on a metaphysical and physical level by his direction, to serve his purpose. That purpose being something, unknown but fortuitous for us all, I pray, that we might now be witnessing with our own eyes!" Cresasern said beaming with joy.

Cresasern's smile and sparkling brown eyes positively lit up in growing hope as he saw, and not imagined he hoped, what could only be described as some kind of a force field deter the killing cloud from taking the two most vulnerable victims in that alley.

"Thank GOD!" Cresasern suddenly shouted, startling his guest sitting quietly over behind the wet bar partaking of a tall mixed drink.

"I am right aren't I? There is something that can stop this evil thing after all? Evil, like science has a limit?" Cresasern asked his silently drinking guest.

"Absolutely boss!" answered Bruno, his large dark brow furrowed up at once in thoughtful speculation.

"One or both of them has it!" Cresasern stated with a finality that even made Bruno take notice.

"Watch over them, on the Q.T. but particularly him, he may be our last, best chance!" Cresasern pleaded seriously.

"Sure," Bruno said, already figuring resolutely deep down in his troubled gut that soon, surely, now he finally was a dead man.

~~~~~

"This is absolutely unfriendly!" Clive shouted loudly, too loudly, causing the moneyed, genteel class people wandering about in the Greenwich borough high-rise's lobby to take unwanted notice of his usually well hidden boorish behavior.

"You're not now nor ever coming up again!" Heda shouted back, adding hot fuel to the rarely seen hereabouts loud uncouth scene parading before the locals.

"I know you, remember, you're no saint!" Clive continued, attempting to touch her face knowingly.

"Back off wanker!" Heda spat hotly as she swatted his hand hard away.

"It's that black American, isn't it?" Clive shrilled, as his oft described handsome face positively blanched a deeper red causing his temple veins to almost positively jump out of his head.

"None of your damn business, you swine! If you come back here again I'll have the coppers on you. That is if I don't shoot you first!" Heda screamed and walked over to the security desk and told the guard there in most adamant terms to put Clive on the permanent verboten list.

"Shoot me---?"

Clive was taken aback at once by this threat as he remembered she did have a BBC provided laser gun and she knew how to use it, and she had done so most effectively on several occasions as he nervously recalled.

Fear changed his rebuffed ego charged ardor to life saving retrospection immediately.

Now, as his one £ pound gram of snorted cocaine ebbed in its frantic effect, cool reason washed over him and he looked around for an escape with some quiet dignity, besides he reckoned that he really should be somewhere else now but fearing that place immensely, he instead stopped here first out of some unfounded hope and sense of forlorn desperation.

With her business finished at the desk Heda left the lobby in a huff, leaving Clive bereft of dignity and solace in the lobby with the upper crust folks gawking at him knowingly, deridingly, since he was sure some of them had to recognize him as a much publicized member of the most important Ministry of Information acting just like a common lout.

Clive thusly self chastised, limped out of the posh residential building fuming and tapping his walking stick nervously, erratically on the building's imported slate floor.

~~~~~

"Been drinking this early in the day? Either you're becoming an Englishman or you're getting old and getting bogged down in life's stark, jarring realities, which is it lad?" Albion queried, wrinkling up his nose as he let Dave into his office.

"A little of both I imagine," Dave answered somberly.

"You decided to take me up on my offer of a heart to heart talk?" Albion asked beaming.

"No!" Dave curtly answered.

"What's up then? What can I do for you? I'm on half day today so can you make it brief?" Albion asked briskly, offering Dave a seat.

"Cresasern sent me," Dave simply stated.

Albion suddenly changed his wavering attitude and at once smiled a wide but suspicious knowing grin.

Dave couldn't believe how much the old fellow's appearance had changed for the better since he had seen him last. Albion's face now exhibited none of the previous sag and blotchiness but now appeared ruddy and glowing.

Albion now stood up straight as he walked about the office and appeared to have lost quite a bit of flabby weight. The man positively exuded good health and well being. Dave jealously wondered what kind of Viagara he was using.

Still Dave didn't like or trust Albion, but Cresasern had given him definite directions.

"I got something for you, "cousin". Payback for that Mellors affair! --- I was told to say all that," Dave simply said pulling out a plastic enclosed disk the size of the American metal quarter coin and handing it over to Albion.

With that Dave got up and left, not caring to wait around for the shit to hit the fan as he knew it certainly would now.

Albion, for his part, simply discretely pocketed the disk and waiting a few minutes, left the building with a song in his heart.

You find your friends where you can. That had been Albion's life's mantra, and it continued to work well for him even now, he noted happily.

Sure he'd informed Cresasern that his employee Mellors had been snuffed at the airport so he could act before others could. He'd also told Cresasern the identities, and particulars tying them to the Ministry of Information of the two goons most recently killed in the alley, thus his gaining his most recent present; the disk.

And why not? The fellow had helped him before in many cases unbeknownst to the powers that be. Albion knew he owed some of his considerable reputation to the help of his unseen, unrecognized ally Benjamin Cresasern.

Arriving home, Albion meant to retreat downstairs to his daily screened "safe room" to view the disk but was stopped by a note left on the kitchen table. Nervously he opened it and read:

> "Dear Egon I've left you for my
>
> gynecologist! I won't be back!
>
> Don't look for me!
>
> Florence."

For a second Albion felt lost, hurt, and angry, then easily, suddenly, a sense of overwhelming calm rationality and happiness pervaded his daily growing stronger body as never before. His new feelings suddenly, unexpectedly, contained a soft spot for both Florence and her gynecologist.

Looking back on it now he realized that he never was her passion like her tea parties, or her committees, or her hobbies. No, he saw now that at best he'd been a good second fiddle to her everything else, he thought, soberly facing troubling facts.

He realized that he was quite happy to be free of her, as he imagined the many new women he could now happily pursue and catch if you believed the odds offered on the "telly" for romance opportunities for a still functioning man his age.

But if he loved Florence as he always assumed he did, then why now was he happy for himself but now growing unhappy for Dr. Phillips her gynecologist? No matter, the world now beckoned to him anew and he intended to grasp it as he grabbed a bottle of Scotch and made his way down past his newly furniture bare house to his cellar and his safe room with the disk clutched in his shaking hand.

~~~~~

Sir Archibald Sleetel loved the Hackney borough with every single one of his three hundred bulging pounds of flab. Actually he thought; I love every hooker in Hackney, everyone that I know that is. This happy thought came to him this dark late evening many hours way past midnight as he left one of his favorite sporting houses; the Aldridge House.

"That was a lot better than spending the evening at the opera with my capricious wife," Sir Archibald Sleetel laughed, remembering happily a most particularly quirky thing he had forced his escort to do earlier, as he slovenly, slowly, weaved his way down the tall staircase.

Mistress of ceremonies this night; a Ms. Sarah Ballallright had just spent the better part of two hours trying arduously and mostly vainly to attempt satisfying Sir Sleetel's more exotic, exhaustingly sickening desires. Finally sated, he left the tired out professional upstairs crying her myriad woes out to her trade sisters who were most happy this night to have escaped his clutches themselves--- this time.

Gaining the foggy street Sir Sleetel spied his big purple limousine, with his sleeping driver Rialto slumped over behind the wheel as usual.

"What---a lazy---bum," Sir Sleetel muttered as he waddled up the deserted, darkened, street toward his transport.

Gaining his car he found the back door locked, so he gingerly knocked on the front passenger side window in order to rouse Rialto.

Suddenly a large gray swirling, tornado of a cloud fast swept loudly banging away up the street behind him from the direction of the sporting house toward the waddling, pounding, Sir Sleetel. This loud disturbance caused him to stop his pounding dead in his tracks, and turning back to see what was approaching him, he wondered aloud, "what in the hell is that?"

The loud, shrilly moaning sound the cloud emanated grew to a deafening pitch and began to frighten Sir Archibald to the utmost as he beheld something that his mind couldn't make sense of swoop down on him.

The fast moving, whirling cloud then smacked right into Sir Archibald hard with a loud series of bone snapping crunches that resonated sickly up and down the street which now contained a single young couple of lovers who had the bad misfortune of just tipsily turning the corner right onto this horrible scene.

They watched utterly transfixed; the man and woman, stuck stark still in their drunken tracks, in awe and fright as the cloud violently lifted up the rotund old man from the street and slammed him this way and that about high in the air. All the while the poor man's harrowing screams were eerily punctuated by the resounding loud whining snarls of the cloud.

The shivering with fear couple could now, despite their inebriation, notice that the violently swirling cloud, as it tossed its victim about, was also cutting him up and shredding his skin in a very gory manner!

They watched in stunned silence as the cloud, its gory work finally done to its satisfaction, with the bloody body now hanging limply in the air, it then shucked what was left of its rotund victim most violently and tossed his bleeding, shredded body onto the rear deck of an opulently painted purple limousine nearby.

The rapidly swirling tornado cloud then with a loud rush of uncommonly loud hellish noises swirled away, in the opposite direction up the street, from the now definitely more sober young couple who now with much surprise saw a uniformed driver timidly exit the limousine to shockingly discover the decidedly shocking bloody mess of a once live human being laying all over his long shiny rear deck!

Chapter 9

Thursday, October 20, 2016

"The good news is that this time we have two and a half witnesses!" Dickett crowed happily while pointing to the van containing the two huddled young people and the half witness as specified, as Albion arrived on the shocking scene this dank, dark night.

"That's different---! What's their story?" Albion asked lazily.

"That's the problem and the bad news; the two, not the half, they both say a tornado did it!" Dickett cried, his hazel eyes flashing wildly with disbelief and exasperation.

Albion didn't flinch a bit, but coolly, coldly, regarded Dickett with a stern, frightened, knowing look never seen before causing a chill to travel up Dickett's broad back.

"Did you keep the press at bay as I asked? They know nothing of the witnesses?" Albion asked, looking about at the rowdy mob growing out on the police periphery.

"Sure! The BBC, they sent over a buzzer spy drone though, but we shot it down!" Dickett crowed as his concern grew.

"Good, that'll certainly give them something to talk about on the morning news," Albion quipped wryly, all the while looking up for more buzzers.

"You did hear me? I said a tornado!" Dickett suspiciously queried, trying to figure out what was going on in Albion's head this night.

"I heard you!" was all Albion said as he went over and entered the van containing the huddled couple sitting inside on one side bench while the other, the swarthy, thin driver, sat forlornly alone on the other looking like a lost sheep. Dickett followed close behind Albion in ignorant curiosity.

"Is that your story?" Albion first asked the shaken up huddled pair.

They both nodded affirmatively, still holding on to each other for dear life.

"Get their statements and their contact particulars, then take them uptown, not too far mind you, and let them go. Don't let the press see them!" Albion ordered the stunned Dickett.

"This one is the half. This here bloke is Rialto Cricilli, Sir Sleetel's supposedly fast asleep driver, an "intercontenental flight to avoid confinement type" I suspect, though his papers appear clear. He says he didn't see "nothing", of course," Dickett reported, nervously gesturing toward the other one; the uniformed driver, sitting alone and shaking away on the other side of the van as far back as he could go.

"I believe him too," Albion smirked, "do the same with him."

Dickett paused, gulped, and then simply nodded in stunned disbelief.

"Listen up you three! You're not to discuss what happened here with anyone! Anyone! Your lives surely depend on it! Do you understand? I'll be in touch with you later!" Albion admonished in an ominous voice that sent chills down even Dickett's back.

The three shocked people nodded in affirmation, at least happy to be understanding that much about what was occurring this night.

Albion exited the van and approached the rear of the limousine containing the remains of Sir Sleetel poorly covered up under a tarp.

Lifting up the green tarp revealed that which ordinarily would have turned his stomach a few months before, now it just more than frightened him. The remains of Sir Sleetel glared back silently, but loudly at the same time, at Albion in obvious testimony to the existence of supernatural evil.

"You can't seriously believe them?" Dickett cried, trying to make some sense out of all the nonsense abounding today.

"Dickett, if you ever see this "tornado" thing coming your way, run like hell!" Albion simply stated.

"You do know something?" Dickett shakily, discretely, asked so no one else could hear.

"I know too much!" Albion stated, heading for his car, leaving Dickett standing in the street with his unease growing by the minute.

~~~~~

The imposing half Gothic, half twisted modern styled building deep in the midst of Westminster City thronged with the hurried pronounced activity of an army of many armed men and women. Walking up the Ministry's steep steps with his official summons tightly clutched in his grasp, Dave felt both fear and unease.

The whole place was awash in bustling armed people as Dave gained the large imposing front door.

The sentry there, a hard, male looking female with machine gun slung under her arm sneered openly his way as she diligently perused his summons and then roughly passed him through to the upright door scanner.

Uniformed, body armored, heavily armed men and women with upraised visors and ready weapons infested the entire place. This entire scene was a repeat, he noted nervously, but with even more jack booted soldiers, of the reception he had received at the airport.

Now Dave began to sweat as the scanner lit up on and above and around him. Cresasern said earlier that the scanner could only pick up that what it already knew about. Dave was about to prove or disprove that theorem, with much nervous concern not readily evident on his part, he hoped.

The scanner lit up and no loud sounds or alarms flashed as it scanned him, and so Dave gave a sigh of relief.

"What's happening?" Dave now asked feeling a bit safer, and braver.

"They'll tell you inside what they want to tell you!" the hard looking guard snarled in a deep bass tone as she passed Dave on to his escort who informed Dave that any false moves on his part would be answered with a burst from the man's ready automatic machine gun. The tall, young, thin man snarled this with such a cold iciness the led Dave to believe that that was an entirely possible occurrence.

Ushered into Sir Reginald's office, Dave came face to face with the three unsmiling men inside.

The armed guard remained close to Dave, so close Dave felt the fellow's tepid bad breath beating hotly on the back of his neck.

Two of the men, the younger ones, inside were seated behind a large wide desk while the third, a particularly old looking gent, hovered about off the floor in a magnetic chair to their left. The man in the hovering chair before him gestured to the single chair placed ominously before the men behind the desk.

"I'm Sir Reginald Bowden, this is Sir Isaac Roland and this is our aide Mr. Clive Waddell. We're glad you could make it," Sir Reginald said while floating easily back and fro, all the while poorly pretending that the summons was a voluntary request.

"Anything I can do to help, well, I'm at your service," Dave said, sitting and quickly scanning around the room for a year in the past as Cresasern had ordered him to.

"Tell us what you know about what happened in that alley Saturday night!" Sir Roland barked nervously.

Dave demurred a minute, thinking; how much do they know?

"Cut the crap! We have witnesses that saw you there!" shouted the youngest one; Clive Waddell, in a high pitched shrill voice that startled all in the room and caused Dave to hear a little bell go off in his head.

"He's right! We know you were there. All we want is some information," Sir Reginald implored acting pitifully.

"I can't help you, I was unconscious," Dave simply and honestly stated just as Cresasern admonished him earlier to do; use the truth. If they accept that then Dave'll know that they used their own device to see what happened and you can then act accordingly in dealing with them.

The three agitated men then conferred amongst themselves for a while as all the while the young blond haired nervous one glowered hatefully at Dave as though they had always been life long enemies, even in a past life.

"What do you think happened and why didn't you go to the police?" Sir Reginald asked sternly, suspiciously, his hovering arc increasing.

I don't rightly know. It's beyond me, what happened, and that's why I didn't go to the police. Fear and dread, and how could I explain something that I didn't see nor if I had, I couldn't explain. Besides, the police already have me on the short shit list in this matter. What would you have done?" Dave answered simply, honestly, knowing full well that they were scanning him even now to determine his veracity with hidden body scanners.

"We ask the questions here!" suddenly shouted Clive even shriller than before.

Now, another bell rang in his head and Dave knew that what ever it was that was troubling these fellows today had more to do with their own personal interests than the fate of those two goons in the alley, for a certainty.

Once again they conferred amongst themselves and then Sir Roland spoke evenly, coldly, "You may go, we'll be in touch if we need you again. Keep the summons! We know where you are!"

Inwardly, Dave breathed a sigh of relief.

The guard then roughly grabbed Dave and hauled him up and out of the room and pushing away with his gun, propelled him all the way through the building till he was pushed out the doorway eliciting a wide smile from the mannish looking woman guard.

Once gaining the freedom of the street Dave proceeded north, quite a few blocks away and downloaded his scans to Cresasern since they both feared that any Wi-Fi transmission in the Ministry building would certainly cause the undoing of their plans and result in immediate incarceration or worse for Dave.

The bells in his brain began ringing anew and it finally began to dawn on Dave why they were chiming so stridently in his mind.

~~~~~

"He was telling the truth that Asher fellow was!" Sir Reginald aptly surmised, exhaling deeply.

"I don't care, I want him and Morgan dead now!" bawled Clive, shrilly.

"I don't care what you want! I give the orders around here and I order you to go back to the alley and scan it again. You didn't do it right!" Sir Reginald shouted at Clive.

Clive fumed, but he needed the brisk air to clear his head for more much needed cocaine consumption so he got up and grabbed the Extraminator device from inside the desk and left still fuming.

After Clive had left Sir Reginald turned to Sir Roland and said, "Thanks for not letting him in on anything."

"He's your problem, but he didn't scan it wrong did he?" Sir Roland responded knowingly, with his brow furrowed in concern.

"No he didn't and I'm not letting him see it! You can see how close to the edge he is and his coke consumption isn't helping him, or us," Sir Reginald explained, swaying about lazily.

Suddenly an armed guard came in and handed Sir Reginald a disk, he having sent the uninformed fellow out earlier to "catch" this, the Sleetel killing, the latest ripping.

Sir Reginald waited until the fellow left and promptly inserted it into a holo-disc player imbedded in his desk and presently the two men watched. Watched in shock and horror, and in three-dimensional holographic clarity, their late colleague Sir Sleetel being shredded to death in much the same fashion that earlier the two had watched their two goons suffer the very same fate.

They knew about this earlier, much earlier, the first proof edition news paper arriving from their own contacts prior to public dissemination.

The blaring early morning headline had read:

"Jack Strikes Back---! He says four down---four to go!--- Sir Sleetel is the latest victim---!"

This news thus necessitated the increased security in the building this morning. They had both decided not to tell Clive anything because they needed him to continue feeling all this was still manageable by him. Telling Clive only that they feared public outcry for banning the use of the Extraminator had, they thought, mollified his limited mind's concerns regarding all the extra guards in the building.

However, what they were seeing now, well, they weren't entirely sure was manageable by any or all of them put together.

As the full sized three dimensional holographic scene of the tornado swirling away and ripping away at Sir Sleetel enfolded and enveloped the two men, they shivered.

"What do you think it is?" Sir Roland asked, his voice visibly quavering.

Sir Reginald shook his head negatively, abjectly, causing his chair to sway erratically.

"You do know who the four left are?" Sir Roland asked rhetorically.

"I reckon!" Sir Reginald barked back nervously.

"How long can you hope to hide it from him?" Sir Roland asked with another twinge of fear snaking into his voice.

"If I knew what that killing thing was, I'd be better able to answer that question," Sir Reginald said, wisely seeing nothing but trouble coming up on his very limited future horizon.

"I'm sleeping here tonight," Sir Reginald said sheepishly.

"I'm not, I intend to see my wife and children once again if this is my end," Sir Roland stated with an air of resignation belying the ominous severity of their situation most succinctly.

~~~~~

Clive exited the limousine, still affecting his fake limp while leaning on his cane in his imagined gentlemanly style, right close after his armed guards. Beheld by benefit of the silver light of the hanging large crescent moon above, the tired, crookedly askew sign swinging precariously above him, proclaiming in loud red scrawl; "Ye Olde Pirate's Roost".

This creepy dockyard pub abutting the Thames just outside the borough of Bexley was just what the doctor ordered, he mused as his men led the way in. First in were the three armed with the automatic machineguns at the ready, behind them flanking Clive strode the two fellows carrying the crunchers.

Once inside the party viewed the boisterously scruffy locals sitting and drinking and carousing as usual. The locals gave the newcomers but a scant cursory glance before resuming their obviously ribald and illegal activities as they wished. Not getting the respectful reaction he'd expected Clive nonetheless looked about for the one that he sought this night.

Spying his target Clive motioned to his guards and they warily made their way through the slowly relenting crowd by forming a moving wedge over to the destination in question. Soon the six men stood ringed before a single figure sitting alone at a small wooden table beside the burning fireplace with a drunken, disheveled, dirty blond haired, ruddy faced whore precariously perched on his knee.

"We need to talk!" Clive shouted above the din.

"I'm done doing your dirty work! You'll need more guards than those this night if you plan trouble with me!" Morgan sneered while sloppily quaffing down his warm mead all the while lasciviously groping the pro's big unhidden breasts.

Clive could barely hide his surprise at seeing Morgan, especially acting in this way. The incongruous sight of Morgan and the whore was shocking Clive's preconceived expectations to smithereens. The ugly fellow was still ugly but now sitting there in his open grey overcoat with his ugly head bare, well, there was definitely something new and refreshingly bizarre about the lout besides his new found floozy friend.

"They're not here for you! They're here for me!" Clive shouted anew.

Morgan now became more interested and rising quickly he caused his bawdy companion to fall drunkenly to the floor as he bade Clive to follow. He led the man into a small room adjacent, and leaving the door slightly ajar in order to watch Clive's guards strode over to the sole table in the room and sat down.

"Talk!" Morgan ordered.

"We need to work together! That thing is coming for us next---!" Clive shouted nervously.

"I've had an epiphany, I don't kill anymore, don't need or want to, and I'm quite resigned to my fate. Besides, I read the papers. I'm waiting for my death! I happily await the angel of death!" Morgan responded coolly.

"Really?" shouted Clive, suddenly releasing his walking stick's three foot long steel shaft and deftly, in a blink, shoving the long blade straight across the table aiming right for Morgan's left eye.

Morgan, instinctively, faster than Clive's eye could discern swerved his head to avoid the blow and standing, unsheathed his own menacing blade. Now the two men warily circled each other as they faced each other over the table both holding sparkling in the dim light steel blades capable of considerable violence at the ready.

"Hypocrite---! Swine! I knew it! You sure act like a man ready to die! Hold on a moment, I have something for you!" Clive laughed as he reached into his pocket and scattered a phone, a holo-disc player, and a small insect on the rickety table before his adversary.

Morgan hesitated as his curiosity grew.

Clive now proceeded to point out the virtues of the items scattered before his "swine" of an adversary.

"This phone is to call me when you come to your senses and you figure out how we together can win! This insect is what the Ministry uses to bug you and me! This player is--- Well just watch!" Clive ordered, pushing the play button on the holo-player.

All at once the small dark room was filled with the vivid scene of the tornado's viciously shredding of the two hired goons.

Morgan and Clive watched in awe; Morgan for the first harrowing time and he couldn't believe his own eyes.

"That there ain't no bloody angel of death! Seems more like a demon from hell to me! These toys are yours. I'd stay away from Bright Gate while playing that disk if I were you. Find somewhere dark under a bridge with the rest of your troll brothers. When you figure out how we together can beat this thing call me! We don't have much time! That is if you suddenly decide to live! Ha---! Clive said retreating backward toward the door with his blade still upraised, extended in Morgan's direction.

Morgan continued to watch in rapt interest as the bloody scene played out again and again before and around him.

"One good thing---!" Clive finished, "We both can continue this fight later; that is if we live. ---I'll be waiting!"

With that he was gone, leaving alone a very troubled Morgan wrestling anew with his own demons.

~~~~~

Dave still couldn't believe his latest spate of what he called good luck but he was sure Cresasern would call blessing, as he reached back and pinched his own bottom with his free right hand, his other busily holding tightly onto Heda's breast.

He snuggled his nose deep into the back of her soft slim almond neck and he shivered as she shivered also. The natural smell of her, and her heady perfume wafted up into his nose and caused him to absolutely suffuse with pleasure all over his body.

Their lunch suddenly turned into an overwhelming lustful desire coming over them both to the extent that they suddenly left their half eaten meals to run over to Heda's flat to satisfy a more pressing need not once but twice.

She pressed her rear cozily into him as she grabbed him again.

This was far and away past pure sex Dave realized as he responded anew and sought out her soft sweet wet lips.

Soon they were doing the dance of love again for the third time.

Later, sated, they lolled sweating against each other on the twisted sheets and both wondered what was happening. This had been totally unplanned, nor expected, especially on her part, and she was quite perplexed, not to mention embarrassed as she sought refuge under the covers.

"Me too!" Dave said happily.

"You too?" she queried with her brown eyes sparkling.

"What do you think is happening?" she asked seriously as her inhibitions came back with a rush.

"Love!" Dave spoke calmly, not questioningly, not believing that he had used the "L" word so easily. For all his adult life he had avoided that word like the plague.

"You've changed!" Heda whispered.

Something odd was happening to him even as he realized it laying here in her arms. He could only describe it a feeling of growth, a feeling of growing strength; spiritual, physical, and intellectual, all at once. Unfortunately, in a flash, Dave at once saw many heretofore hidden past events and things clearly that downright disturbed him but couldn't at all be ignored. Whatever this metamorphosis was, and that's the salient word coming into his mind even now, it reminded him of the overwhelmingly strengthening of his entire body he had felt when he had his last Tetanus shot only this was much stronger. A sense of such strong, growing enhancement caused him to ask her about it as best he could word it.

"Me too!" she responded.

Grabbing her in his arms he pulled her close and they both enjoyed something unexpectedly new and good.

~~~~~

Saturday, October 22, 2016

Sir Roland's entourage of limousines pulled up before his London home in the Islington borough on Slaterly Street around ten o'clock this clear Saturday night. The gentrified street still bustled with quite a few people walking about as the three long black SUVs bristling with armed men blocked traffic as they brazenly crowded traffic on the genteel street as usual.

Walking within and between a brace of some ten armed men Sir Roland felt pretty safe. His escorts this night were armed with the requisite machine guns, laser rifles, and also powerful "crunchers" and they all confidently felt able to handle anything except a small army this night.

Walking toward his home, within the armed mob, they nearly reached but the curb when they heard it---!

It rose in sound and fury before they saw it!

"Look there!" shouted Sir Roland's head security chief; the dark haired, craggy faced Irishman, Ian McCallister, pointing abruptly a ways up the street, to something he saw some twenty feet away.

They all turned and beheld the screaming, twisting, twirling, twenty foot tall grey tornado cloud rapidly swooping down upon them.

Sir Roland immediately lost his lunch and his water in fright as he stood transfixed unable to move.

"Fire!" shouted McCallister loudly, punctuating his strident order to his game lads with a long burst of his own ready machinegun.

Soon, all were firing in an oft practiced manner at the approaching twisting thing. The effect of their considerable throwing of lead and hot laser blasts was only it seemed, the frightful tearing up of the residential street with their usually effective gunfire.

Both the laser beams and the bullets seemed to pass right through the cloud unhindered. The street was lit up like a Christmas tree with the tracers and bright yellow laser blasts flashing up the walkways and careening off the buildings. Street passersby though weren't lucky at all this night as many were seen to fall under the barrage of collateral gunfire while others ran for dear life.

"Crunch it!" yelled McCallister seeing that the small arms fire wasn't stopping the thing coming on them fast one whit.

Now the "cruncher" carrying men came up abreast and resolutely bringing their long black tube weapons to bear on the thing, let them loose on the cloud which now was only some ten feet away and closing rapidly.

Whump, whump, whump, went the crunchers as all looked on with much concern as fear now slowly pervaded, for the first time ever, the ranks of such highly trained men as these.

The manned "cruncher" weapons, the four of them, shot out their electrically charged sound waves in a well practiced powerful volley simultaneously at the wildly twisting cloud.

McCallister now smiled widely because he knew beyond a shadow of a doubt that nothing on this earth could stand up to that kind of concentrated power, that knowledge he would stake his life on, he thought for an instant.

The concentrated charges hit the twister head on and then---!

Then the cloud somehow, McCallister didn't have time to figure out how, held the charges momentarily then shot the four electrified charges right back at the unsuspecting armed body of men. The forceful electric charges came back fast from whence they came from, faster many shaken witnesses would say later, and caused pure hellish havoc on the stalwart skirmish line of defenders this night.

The sound induced electrically charged charges hit them hard and tossed many screaming men about as it also hit the large, heavy SUVs behind them with such force, and a shuddering series of crashes and with screeching sounds that easily pushed them all up onto the curbs crashing into themselves to finally rest here and there willy-nilly.

Armed men went flying now as the cloud hit behind the charges. Now, pure hell reigned on the once peaceful street as the hateful, twisting cloud picked up the sniveling Sir Roland, McCallister, and three of the once well armed men in its killing clutches. The five yelling victims were all swept up and twirled around and shredded horribly while still alive to the frightened stares of the survivors on the ravaged street containing both armed men and hapless local citizenry stuck in their tracks.

A small group of the armed survivors still standing now fled before this thing that they couldn't understand nor handle now as best they could.

Two of them foolishly, bravely they would hope to later tell their grandchildren, stopped momentarily far up the street and fired back once more at the growling cloud that now began discarding its dead shredded victims onto the street as bloody corpses where ever it pleased.

Finding their belligerent activity totally pointless, the men ceased firing and grabbing up a fallen wounded comrade joined the locals in the mad flight of a fear frenzied mob to escape what ever that thing was that cleared the once bustling street tonight so easily.

Chapter 10

Monday, October 24, 2016

"Five down, three to go---!" Jack warns after creating mayhem on Slaterly Street!---Sir Roland is the latest victim---!" the Evening Standard blared loudly.

"Give me some more of that!" shouted Sir Reginald, referring to one of the lines of coke Clive was busily setting up.

Clive laughed as he eagerly offered up some coke to his now broken, shaken, shell of a once formidable boss.

Snorting the powdery white stuff for the first time, Sir Reginald at once felt the first pleasurable rush as he remembered back:

It was on a dark gloomy night, in this very room, the assembly court, some two months before that the three of them, the all powerful, had over brandy and cognac hatched their once so simple plot. Sleetel, Roland and he had huddled, groused, fumed, and finally plotted the plot that now not only came back to bite them but it looks; to eat them.

"They've taken our energy income!" Sleetel had drunkenly groused.

"They've cut me out of my shipping monopolies!" Roland complained.

"That whore Trinny Simpson laughed at me!" Reginald whined.

Finally all stinking drunk, they all conspired to right their perceived wrongs by resorting to murder. Kill the three they wanted dead the most and blame it on Black Science. What could be simpler or more effective? At least that's what they thought at the time.

Sleetel wanted Elbert Stoner dead for working with Black Science and thus stopping his once lucrative fossil fueled energy income. The minor union official had loudly advocated using anything that cursed new science offered to cut Sleetel and his thugs out of their old positions of controlling the oil wells and distribution channels.

Roland complained that he wanted Sir Arthur Claypool dead for interfering in his shipping concerns on the docks. Actually he hated the man for employing hundreds of "catchers" in the ancient Library of Alexandria and digging up so much long thought lost human knowledge and information, information that in time would make hundreds of his company's patents obsolete. He hated the nerve, the audacity of them to put mankind's welfare above his own need for profit!

Sir Reginald stated that he wanted Trinny Simpson dead because of his misogynist hatred and her lack of vigorous cooperation in meeting his sexual needs. In actuality he was pissed that she had given his only son two things; one a death sentence, the other, the lesser one of which was curable, he hoped; a serious heroin addiction.

Kill them all and blame it on Jack the Ripper and Black Science; that had been the plan, and it had worked up to a point, Sir Reginald thought. Well, that point had passed and now of the three left; one original planning member and their two unsuspecting minions; these two of them now huddled together seeking solace in drugs.

Sir Reginald could hear the bustle of the armed guards rushing around the building and he knew that this would be a most eventful day. The Prime Minister had stepped in and called a conference for today to sort all this out. There would be no sweeping last night's massacre on Slaterly Street under the rug.

"Give me another hit!" Sir Reginald ordered, knowingly realizing he'd surely be requiring all the real or false courage he could muster today; this day the general assembly was to meet to hopefully plan a strategy for stopping that infernal tornado cloud menace.

Clive avidly watched the old geezer snort away with an evil rapt attention etched on his square face that the old man missed noticing, so mired in his own troubles. The old, short, grizzled scion of old line British aristocracy and secretive Norman Council power; lost in his own fears, missed the point that Clive's incessant strident whining of late was now replaced with a calm conniving evil attitude.

Sir Reginald winced at the thought of those people who soon would be crowding into these hallowed walls and filling these seats at the conference table. People he wouldn't even speak to, the unworthy, those he wanted dead.

The dreaded, despised, Benjamin Cresasern came readily to mind with a blinding flash of hate as well as Prime Minister "P.M." Willa Chambers. Willa the dumb they called her, picked her for that very reason they did; another plot coming back to bite him, he groused. Willa would do the bidding of the council, too dumb to realize her role as the beard she was. Whatever odious aim the council wanted they made Willa front it, if it worked they took the credit, if it didn't she took the heat and she still wasn't the wiser.

The cocaine soon began soothing Sir Reginald's nerves and he dismissed Clive to face his own personal firing squad alone in about a half hour.

~~~~~

Dave watched Cresasern fairly bubble with glee.

They were up in the headquarters building and Cresasern was surrounded with his retinue of tailors fitting him out in Saville Row dark grey wool this day for his meeting soon with the mucky-mucks over at the Ministry building.

Meanwhile the overhead ticker printed out: "Shuttle Explorer 1 unmanned mechanical probe to Alpha-2 space station finds all eleven crew dead; green fungus growing out of control, extraterrestrial spores from Saturn's moon Enceladus suspected!.....30 die as poor riot in NYC, Miami, and Detroit again, cause: outsourcing exceeds domestic job production by 50%!.....China strikes North Korean reactor with coordinated air strikes!.....Massive world wide civilization threatening asteroid discovered with an intersecting Earth orbit in 2026!"

"You've done us another good turn," Cresasern chortled, slapping Dave hard on the back and toppling over one of his less agile tailors.

Taking Cresasrn's seemingly good humor as a good omen Dave smiled while wondering what was next.

"We now know who is behind this whole mess! That is we know who's left of the original cabal!" Cresasern shouted happily.

"Your scan showed us everything except who did the actual Ripper killings," Cresasern said, now admonishing a tailor on the too long cut of his cuff.

"No matter, the cloud knows," Dave said snidely.

"Actually, you're right," Cresasern echoed, taking a good long questioning staring look at Dave, as if seeing him for the first time.

"What?" Dave asked noticing the long stare.

"You've changed!" Cresasern noted, regarding Dave with an unexpected proud smile.

"Somebody else said that same thing to me just a while ago," Dave answered proudly, but still he felt the confusion grow inside himself.

"Don't let your first baby steps turn your head!" Cresasern admonished, wincing as he was stuck in the leg by a nervous haberdasher.

"What do you mean?"

"Some of us never know our higher purpose. Some of us don't have a purpose, and never will. You may be one of the few of us that won't suffer either of those fates. All I can say now is I have high hopes for you. Your job is to go with the flow wherever it takes you. Got that?" Cresasern said seriously, giving Dave a firm pat on the shoulder.

~~~~~

Storm clouds slowly formed ominously over New Scotland Yard while inside, on the fourth floor; and as the lights came on, the sharp loud raps on the blackboard behind Albion on his right resounded to quiet his understandably troubled roll call this morning.

The explicit film provided this day, shaky as it was, was provided by a local resident of Slaterly Street having the courage and foresight to record the macabre happenings, in situ, despite much fear to life and limb.

"See here," he shouted as he slapped the unchanged blackboard still holding the same pictures it had the last roll call.

"Jack's stopped the progress here!" Albion quipped snidely.

"Should we still try to apprehend those responsible for the original killings?" asked Sergeant Craig Oliver, glancing over behind a row of blue at the always well hidden Dickett trying to get ever smaller over in the corner. .

"No let "Jack" handle them!" Albion barked, almost starting a mutiny in the ranks that is if the negative outcry could be believed.

"Now take heed and remember what I'm saying to you this day on pain of death! Albion shouted while loudly rapping away on the other blackboard; the one behind and on his left with the growing list of pictures and notes of the "real", or tornado Ripper's victims.

"See these folks? They took on something that can't be stopped! You just saw the film!" Albion cried.

With that the room erupted anew with shouts of fear and concern and a few nervous snickers.

"We haven't a chance of stopping whatever it is, least wise arresting it!" Albion shouted to the group, especially to the few nervous snickers in the room.

"This isn't easy for me either, I didn't believe in demons either, like most of you, until I saw this film!" Albion continued. "My orders to you all are; if you see it coming try to get anyone in the area to leave immediately, barring that, leave yourselves immediately! You hear?"

"You mean retreat?" suddenly asked Albion's perennial scapegoat Officer Iris Muldoon, half-standing, in her gratingly squeaky voice.

"Sure, that is unless you have handcuffs big enough to span a twenty foot tall tornado!" Albion responded causing her to sit her trim frame down to the nervous guffaws of her comrades.

"Run like hell, until they, you know the Government, or the military, come up with something new, we can't fight it. You saw the film; lasers, gunfire, crunchers; all to no effect! We don't have a nuke and I doubt that would work either!" Albion said sadly, at once feeling quite old and impotent again.

Unfortunately his advice to run, well, that was the best that Albion could offer as yet, since the various police scientists including Dr. Griscom, and even Professor Billingsly who had seen this film and the disk created by Cresasern, to date haven't come up with a definitive scientific explanation for understanding or combating the tornado demon.

~~~~~

Clive cursed. The hypocrite wouldn't answer the phone. He'd been trying to reach Morgan for near two days to no avail.

Leaving the Ministry building with his guards in tow, Clive fumed about that and something else. Yesterday he saw on the street Heda and the black American walking together. They had been holding hands! Holding hands! How dare she? That really hurt! Clive fumed raising his blood pressure.

This called for drastic action, Clive vowed as he made his way southwest to the laboratory of Buttermind Industries in the Wandsworth borough. Clive had a friend there, one who owed him, one with the steel trap brain of a genius but the morals of an alley cat. She could help him here if Morgan wouldn't or couldn't, Clive just knew; while patting his vest pocket containing the package and cocaine she would most surely require to comply with his wishes.

She viewed the disc showing the alley shredding over and over while Clive stood amidst the unfolding holographic image and admired her full figure lustfully and wondered why he'd broken up with her anyway.

"Intersting! Very interesting," Beatrice McAdams repeated as she wiped her reddening, running nose with her sleeve.

"Can you tell me anything?" Clive pleaded, pulling her close and smelling her heady perfume started to think of rekindling their romance if that's what you wanted to call it. Actually, he now recalled, it had been pure sex in the beginning, nothing more on either of their parts, but she wanted more after a while and Clive wouldn't have that.

"What's in it for me?" she asked pulling away immediately.

Clive then pulled out the package and offered it up to her while putting on his best rake's grin.

She opened it and squealed loudly.

"You should have!" she crowed as she turned her back to him so Clive could fasten the expensive diamond and ruby necklace to her neck.

That done, the rebuffed Clive tried to grasp her again but she slipped away easily and stood aloof before him and wagging her finger warned, "Once bitten twice shy! I will tell you this; those two, the prone ones, they are the key to your dilemma!"

Clive perked up at once.

"What---?"

"That thing went straight for them too but something stopped it in its tracks, like it hit a brick wall of sorts. I'd say they can stop it! Somehow---!" she stated referring to the unconscious Heda and Dave as the disc had shown, while admiring her necklace in a mirror.

"Show me! Now---!" Clive barked, grabbing Beatrice and pulling her close, while a desperate plan slowly formed in his twisted jealous mind that might just work to solve all of his present problems.

~~~~~

"Let me get this straight! You want us, the Black Science community; a community you have limited, derided and persecuted and I might add, prosecuted for years, to formulate a weapon to stop this avenging creature---for you?" Cresasern shouted angrily.

Ten years ago Cresasern and his fellow black comrades were hiding in safe houses and caves to escape jail and the usurpation of their inventions and the profits inherent. Now rich; they lived above ground and kept their former persecutors on the run as much as they could. Those ten years underground, though, still chafed at many, especially Cresasern, thus his anger today.

Willa Chambers, P.M., taking her cue from the sleazily swarthy Sir Stephan Wiley sitting to her right; the architect of the many horns of the cuckold now perched prominently on her husband's head, said, "I know in the past we've had our differences, but I was hoping that you came here, in the spirit of cooperation, to help."

Benjamin Cresasern looked about the massive room at the thirty or so people gathered at the modern round table, many of them probably armed, and the forty heavily armed guards standing behind them ringing the room's walls and shivered. Glancing up at the steel barred windows above let him know that someone in this room was very concerned with staying alive and Cresasern thought he knew who it was.

"You haven't answered the question!" Cresasern shouted.

"The answer is yes!" she answered huffily, feeling very embarrassed before the group today and having to take low to this pompous black fellow whom she never thought she'd have to talk to, much less never, never, have to beg from ever in life.

"Do you want the good news first or the bad news first?" Cresasern asked quite satisfied by getting her to kneel to something other than her own upper-crust vanities.

Willa once again shifted her eyes to Sir Wiley who discretely showed her two fingers.

"The bad news!" she happily, ignorantly, then crowed to the abject but hidden disdain of all the thirty or so dignitaries both political and military, in the assembly room ringed around the massive round oak table.

"The bad news is that tornado thing, which we all now think is a real demon from hell, exists, as well as we have determined, in both this physical world and also in the spiritual, the metaphysical world, obeying, or disobeying whatever laws of both worlds it requires as it wills! There is nothing that man can or has ever created in this world that can stop it!" Cresasern said sadly.

Willa, not at all pleased with that, went on with a dumfounded expression on her plain, square, over powdered dull face, with, "and the good news?" This she delivered in such a much practiced solicitous tone so as to be almost insulting.

"The good news is that when the evil creature is done getting those that it wants, it'll probably leave!" Cresasern stated confidently while looking dead on at Sir Reginald Bowden who sat directly across the table from him floating about more nervously than usual.

Sir Reginald returned Cresasern's cold stare with a feeble one of his own from under his bushy grey eyebrows as best he could muster this day given the euphoria he still felt from the cocaine.

Willa and the entire assemblage at the table weren't too happy with Cresasern's prognosis at all and began to confer angrily amongst themselves along party lines and affiliations.

"There's more good news!" Cresasern suddenly shouted, quieting the tumult to a quiet din.

"What is it?" Sir Wiley asked speaking out of turn.

"We can pray that Jesus Christ will intercede with GOD on our behalf!" Cresasern stated in a strong tone.

The assemblage stared, dismissively gawked, and then went back to squabbling amongst themselves as Cresasern and Sir Reginald stared at each other across the massive table ignoring all others.

Their stare match was suddenly interrupted by a rushing, loud tumultuous sound enveloping from above, as though a freight train was fast approaching the building. Naturally all the others stopped bickering as the noise grew louder and more deafening.

~~~~~

Dave sat on a large marble bench in the Ministry hallway awaiting Cresasern's return from the meeting inside. They were making a lot of raucous noise inside and he and the guards standing here in the corridor could barely stifle their snickers at the bombastic rumblings of the powerful emanating from inside.

"It's always like this," snorted one of the guards, the younger one with the shock of blond hair bursting out from under his too large helmet.

"Can it! Are you daft?" shouted the other one, flanking the other side of the massive double doors, to his errant mate.

Suddenly a young man ran up to them and tried to get into the room. He was restrained by the guards but he was agitated and adamant.

"I'm Clive Waddell, you know me! I've an urgent message for Sir Reginald Bowden!" Clive shouted in that shrill tone that Dave remembered now from the night he was pushed out the window.

That shrill voice conjured up the bad memory of being thrown out the window and Dave rose along with his out of control anger to confront the fellow and find out what was he up to now.

Clive, recognizing Dave sneered, "What are you doing here?"

"None of your damn business, you wanker!" Dave shouted back picking up some local slang, and grabbing Clive by the collar, he reared back his fist to strike the fellow.

"Here, none of that!" shouted the older guard restraining Dave with an arm lock.

Clive easily slipped out of Dave's restrained grasp, causing the agitated fellow to back up a bit, quite confused and flustered now, and then he went back to trying to get in the room.

"I have to get in there!" Clive wailed to the unrelenting guards who responded with, "when they're through mate!"

"I'm not your damn mate!" Clive shouted shrilly.

Suddenly the arguing men in the corridor heard it!

The loud rushing freight train sound started and soon it sounded as though it was right outside the building. It frightened all of them as all of a sudden the building actually violently shook to its core with a loud crashing sound. The shaking building toppled the men in the corridor to the floor and as they slowly rose in stunned disbelief the large red double doors before them opened out with a deafening crash and out flew a good fifteen or so dignitaries and guards who trampled the surprised men in the hall, knocking them about again onto the floor, in their mad rush to be somewhere, just not there.

Then the large double doors rang closed with a whoosh and a sharp crash of its metal hardware and the ominous sounds of gunfire and cries of human pain and anguish emanated from the closed room to the stunned fear of those outside.

Dave rushed to the door as did Clive. Between them they couldn't open it, no matter how hard they tried. Motioning to the two guards for help, the one; the young one came over while the other one ran out of the building as fast as he could.

The three desperate men now wrestled with the door as they heard the loud sounds of mayhem inside grow in intensity. The loud cries of many obviously distressed people increased. The gunfire continued, the crunching continued as the whirling sound did also. Still the door didn't give.

As soon as it started it stopped! The rushing sound stopped! The gunfire stopped! Now all that could be heard inside the room was one single sound; a redundant thumping noise as though someone was banging on a wall.

Dave and Clive thus attempted to open the door anew; the young guard was now not so sure that's what he really wanted to do as he retreated backwards quite a bit.

It was then that they were joined by a giant of a man who pushed them both aside and grabbed the door's ringed knockers and pulled along with them. Dave smiled up at Bruno and received a grim grin in return.

"Surprised?" Bruno asked simply.

"Not in the least!" Dave answered putting his back into it.

They then opened the door surprisingly easily and beheld the wrecked room. It certainly looked like a tornado had gone through it. Everywhere laid the debris of the once finely furnished assembly room; walls, columns, tables, chairs, curtains, all askew and broken as if by a whirlwind. Blood splatter liberally sprinkled the walls and ceiling, dripping down ominously.

Wounded and dead people were lying about all over the place. Above, the steel encased windows hung in shredded reams while below the plaintive moans of the injured grew.

As Dave frantically searched; he also wondered why he was overly concerned about Cresasern's condition, but before he could plumb that question adequately, he found Cresasern lying motionless under the shattered round table wounded badly, barely breathing, but happily still alive.

As Bruno barked into his ear bud comm-link for ambulance services and as the room began to fill with guards and rescue personnel Dave did that which he knew Cresasern required of him, and would probably fire and then kill him if not done well. Dave scanned the room back a good hour and hoped Cresasern would live to see it someday.

Clive, avidly following the source of the thumping sound, frightfully spied Sir Reginald over against the far section of the room. His lifeless body hung in tatters as his floating chair swayed this way and that in the air bumping dumbly into the far wall slamming his bloody, shredded body roughly about with every resounding thump!

Chapter 11

Monday, October 24, 2016

Albion finished gathering their statements, such as they were, from those able to give them from the ragged bunch of lightly wounded people scattered about on the sloping well manicured lawn before the wrecked Ministry building.

From these happy survivors he learned what he could and then approached Dave and Bruno tiredly sitting under a tree quietly watching each other warily.

Plopping himself down heavily on the bench with them Albion began with, "four dead, seven touch and go including Cresasern."

"It could have been worse," Dave remarked solemnly.

Albion watched as the last of the robots removed the dead, the wounded having already been evacuated to hospital first and asked, "You fellows got anything to add to your statements?"

"No!" they both answered in unison.

"Where's that Clive Waddell bloke? I haven't got his statement. He was here---right?" Albion asked looking about warily.

Dave looked about also and not seeing the swine anywhere he once again noticed that bell began to ring in his head.

"He was here," Bruno said flatly.

"I'll take one more look about, and then I'll run you lads down to hospital with me," Albion said getting up to canvass anew.

"How long?" Bruno asked once Albion was out of earshot.

"Ever since Cresasern and his goons held a gun against your head in the bathroom," Dave simply responded.

Bruno gave him a look of total confusion.

"Cresasern; he knew your name," Dave explained nonchalantly.

"Think you're bright? Huh?" Bruno asked snidely.

"Getting there," Dave returned sarcastically.

"OK. I've been working with him for a good while. So what?" Bruno huffed defiantly.

"No matter. I don't trust either of you now. You two always have something sinister going on. I wouldn't be surprised if you both didn't have the slightest idea what you're really about. You're the only comedy team I know without at least one straight man." Dave complained while getting up to join Albion waving by his car.

The drive downtown to hospital was an icy one.

Saint Alban's emergency room bustled with the overflow from the Ripper's latest strike. The harried place boomed with the sounds of rushing, shouting doctors and patient's anguished cries as never before.

The P.M., Wiley, Cresasern, and the rich had long since been moved upstairs to private quarters. Those left here below were the poorer, less critically injured, less insured ones.

Cresasern lay doped up in his bed with a not ugly, at all but quite pretty, busty, fake blond haired Asian looking and sounding nurse by his bedside. Dave figured her to be his privately paid retinue.

"He's been shot!" Albion remarked dryly, "the tornado thing didn't lay a hand or whatever on him."

"On purpose?" Bruno asked, with his dark brow furrowed in suspicion.

"We may never know. The recording cameras in the assembly room were all fried," Albion said sadly.

"Why aren't you up in the penthouse seeing about your P.M.?" Dave rudely asked Albion.

"She's not one of my friends and that fellow there is! Besides she has her MI-5, Bond types up there, I'd only be in the way--- if they let me in! Her only injuries are those she sustained when her boyfriend Wiley fell on her anyway." Albion answered back fast, pointing to Cresasern, causing Dave to feel ashamed of his rude, flippant attitude.

Suddenly the over head TV blared out in staccato causing all in the room to take notice: "Jack strikes again! This time at the Ministry of Information! Seven injured! Four dead, including Sir Reginald Bowden! P.M. Willa Chambers not gravely injured! Jack says to Evening Standard: "six down, two to go!"

"Two left, I wonder who they are?" Albion asked, looking questioningly at both Dave and Bruno.

"I think I know one of them," Dave said smirking, suddenly noticing Cresasern weakly opening his eyes.

The man on the bed feebly motioned Dave over and bade him move closer for a whisper in the ear.

Dave timidly did so and so soon heard only the soft raspy gurgle of a sound from the man of what once used to be a strong baritone.

"Take what the nurse has for you! It'll all become clear to you later!" Cresasern firmly, but feebly mumbled and then fell asleep under the influence of the drugs administered earlier.

The busty Asian nurse swayed her hips a bit too wildly for nursing to be her only profession as she came over and gave Dave an envelope which he nervously took and suspiciously regarded as Bruno and Albion watched him hungrily in much the fashion as would vultures over a new kill all the while wondering what it contained.

~~~~~

Clive cursed anew; the swine still wouldn't answer the phone. To hell with him, groused Clive as he and his crew sped through the streets of London toward Greenwich. With sirens blaring loudly, the car wildly cleared away a path of luckily flying pedestrians.

He now knew what he must do and wouldn't let anyone stop him because he knew at the outside he had less than two days, that's how long between the Ripper kills. The desperate men in the petrol powered Maybach had watched the news as had thousands if not millions.

Clive still counted himself lucky because he was the only one in the car who knew who the killer tornado was after. He speculated nervously that if his ignorant crew in the car knew the demon wanted him; only him and Morgan, well he was sure they'd desert him immediately, the four of them.

Also if they knew what that tornado thing really was they'd desert fast. Best to keep them in the dark as long as possible he slyly figured as they pulled up with a screech of rubber in front of Heda's Greenwich borough high-rise.

"Shoot anyone in the place that gets in our way lads!" Clive shrilly ordered as they all piled out of the car and rushed into the building, roughly scattering about the folks outside walking a mite too slow for them this day.

~~~~~

"OK what is this?" Dave asked as he followed Bruno into Cresasern's Westminster office.

"It's the combination of this safe!" Bruno said, passing a massive hand over a painting of John Brown on the far wall causing the picture to rise revealing the wall safe in question.

"Well, go on!" Bruno ordered.

"Why me?" Dave simply asked nervously, quite overwhelmed with what was happening.

"I thought you was so smart! You haven't figured that out yet?" Bruno deeply laughed in his Jersey vernacular.

Dave looked coldly back at Bruno in confusion.

Bruno shook his head in despair, and said, "I still think it's too soon for you, but then again, I'm not the boss," Bruno stated tersely.

Angered for some unknown reason by Bruno's condescending attitude Dave gave Bruno another cold icy glance and bravely went over to the safe and following instructions soon flung it open. Inside it contained but a single manila envelope. Dave opened it but stopped short of revealing its contents; noticing Bruno leaving.

"I'll be outside, that's for you only," Bruno said smiling.

Dave opened the manila envelope and removed its contents and sitting down at Cresasern's desk he started to decipher the cryptic message left by his hospitalized, enigmatic boss as best he could.

~~~~~

Heda and her mom's holographic image were both enjoying their usual Thursday early evening meal for once. Inviting the old woman up to her flat had so far proven more enjoyable than expected, but it was still early, Heda speculated happily.

Heda's overhead TV news link broadcast loudly: "Jack still looking for last two targets!....U.N. team attaches two Jupiter rockets to Space Station Alpha-2 to rocket it into the Sun!.....Resolution requiring political candidates to take written test for ethics, intelligence, and competence held up in U.S. Republican controlled Congress!"

"So how's the American working out?" mum asked as she flickered away across the table.

The woman had no sense of anyone else's privacy or tact, Heda noted, sipping her piping hot coca tea.

"He seems to be a good prospect," Heda simply responded.

"He's black, is he?" mum asked as she began nervously picking at her salad, "your uncle Hamid is going to have another heart attack."

"And a Christian?" mum clucked on.

"I do believe," Heda answered stifling a snicker.

"Have you slept with him yet?" mum blurted out suddenly.

"Do you ever want to get another invite mum?" Heda asked, knowing her cheeks were turning a deep crimson.

"I don't understand you young people at all," mum continued now avidly attacking her curry in New Delhi.

Suddenly Heda's apartment's front door smashed in with the loud sound of a "cruncher" on full blast, followed immediately close behind by a slew of armed guards in front of Clive.

Heda instinctively, immediately bolted and left the table running for her bedroom and her laser gun. The armed men, though expecting that, grabbed her tightly betwixt them restraining her firmly and stood her before the shaking with rage Clive Waddell who regarded her and the image of her mum with not the slightest bit of undisguised malice.

"What in the hell is this about?" Heda shouted angrily, "you got a warrant?"

"We're way past warrants now!" Clive fumed.

"You evil villain, you're breaking the law!" mum shouted as she flickered more haphazardly.

"You're coming with us!" Clive barked to the wildly struggling Heda, "best not resist, you'll only get hurt!"

"Leave my baby alone!" shouted mum stridently.

"Piss off crone!" Clive shouted as he pulled out a very large Luger machine pistol and let loose a hot leaded burst at mum's holographic image across the table. The bullets though, passed right through the flickering image and only tore up the wall behind so Clive then angrily turned the weapon on Heda's holographic phone device with a wanton vengeance that shocked all in the apartment.

As Clive's bullets smashed into the device mum flickered once and again for the last time and then she disappeared in a blast of acrid gun smoke.

"She'll get you good for that!" Heda shouted as the armed men roughly led her out of the apartment with the Luger wielding Clive bringing up the rear reaching now for his ear phone.

~~~~~

Morgan had easily made his decision after seeing the news reports about the killings at the Ministry. With much anger, and satisfaction, he gleefully smashed underfoot the phone Clive had given him with a loud crunch which reverberated off his cell's walls like a clap of thunder.

His remaining time he intended to spend doing better things than futilely aiding that government criminal, he thought happily. Now more sure than ever that resisting that thing was a waste of time, a calm sense came over Morgan. Knowing that death was closing in gave him a freedom that he'd never felt before.

Of course, taking Clive along with him appealed immensely to Morgan, but why do that himself when the creature would do it anyway, and much more painfully it would appear, he laughed. Still, he sure wanted to kill Clive before he left this earth more than anything.

"Be still my heart," Morgan whispered humbly to hopefully rid himself of that nagging thought which only served to get in his way of enjoying his final hours.

A morning of heavy drinking and sexing now finished, Morgan was determined to work and pray around the abbey until nightfall. At that time he would go out in the fields behind the abbey and await his fate, sure as he was that the demon wouldn't dare come inside the abbey.

Of course, Morgan now realized the demon's timetable certainly wasn't his, and how silly a thought that had been. Besides, this fake abbey couldn't offer sanctuary to anyone, Morgan decided sadly.

Suddenly, as if in answer to his present thoughts, an extremely loud commotion erupted from downstairs, and amid the rising shouts of the abbey residents, Morgan knew it had come for him, so he resolutely adjusted his cloak and stuck his knife in the folds of a sleeve and then he went down the stairs to meet his fate with a wry smile on his misshapen face.

The sudden sound of mixed gunfire below surprised him because he knew that he was the only person in the abbey possessing a firearm, which he kept hidden out near the well.

Entering the great room below Morgan was stunned to see Clive and his armed guards rushing into the place firing away at the frantically escaping monks and acolytes, and they, Clive's crew had a girl in tow; a pretty girl in a mauve pantsuit, still she appeared to be an obvious unwilling prisoner.

"What's going on here?" Morgan barked.

"This here bird is one half of the shield we're gonna use against that tornado thing! I reckon it won't be long before the other half of the shield shows up with that thing close behind! We can beat it with your help!" Clive yelled.

"You haven't a chance! Madman!" Heda shouted defiantly kicking at her tormentor's crotch.

Clive responded with a sharp, stinging backhand that stopped her for a while.

"I don't care anymore," Morgan stated solemnly, "I'm not going to do anything to help you!"

"Then you're gonna die now!" Clive shouted as he unexpectedly launched himself right onto the bigger man.

Morgan had waited and wanted this very thing for so long that he absolutely cried with joy as Clive attacked him. Quick as lightening, Morgan reached into his robe and produced his menacing blade in his right hand. Clive, for his part, grabbed Morgan's long massive arms, above the wrists, in his own and leered oddly at his old adversary.

"Surprise!" Clive shouted as he wrenched both his hands around, and as easily as he would crack a peanut he broke both of Morgan's arms mid length up the radius and ulna bones, above the wrists with a loud sick staccato snapping sound that stunned everyone in the room.

Morgan yelled loudly in pain and anguish as he beheld his useless arms dangling grotesquely about before him with the blade still grasped in his closed right hand. Clive then picked Morgan up and flung him against the far wall as easily as though he was a rag doll.

Heda looked on in obvious disbelief as did Clive's stunned guards.

"I.G.F. Insulin Growth Factor! I have the strength of six big men!" Clive crowed as he went over to his shaken guard holding it and retrieved his walking stick, and doing so soon unsheathed its long sharp blade.

All watched with rapt interest as this unexpected drama played out to their utter surprise and fascination.

"Since you don't appear to be much help to me, or to yourself today you'll just have to go!" Clive sneered as he approached and viciously thrust his blade into Morgan who was lying twitching, moaning, and helpless against the wall. The blade struck the whimpering man in the chest above his heart hard and Clive eagerly pushed it on through, smiling wildly all the time.

~~~~~

Dave and Bruno grabbed a sky cab and headed back downtown to Saint Alban's.

Bruno noticed Dave wasn't as argumentative as before and wanted to ask him a few burning questions, but wisely thought better of it.

"Heda's not answering. All I get is that her line is out of order," Dave said tapping his ear phone, with a twinge of concern crossing his face.

"Why are we going back?" Bruno asked.

"I need to hear something," Dave stated, "then I'm swinging by Heda's flat--- alone!"

Bruno chafed a bit at that rebuff, silently though.

Cresasern's private hospital room was bathed in a soft orange light as Dave let himself in. The pert Asian nurse sat over in the corner reading out loud, in Japanese, from a small book and gave him but a glance and a smile as he entered and approached the bed. The room contained, beside the requisite guards, a few of Cresasern's staff all toiling away at a makeshift desk in the far corner.

Cresasern was wide awake and motioned for her to stop with a wave of his hand.

"I read your message; do you really believe crap like that?" Dave asked trying to maintain his temper.

Cresasern regarded him forlornly and said only, "I hope Bruno is wrong about you."

"You have to get all the hate out of you in order to become what I suspect you can be! Forgive your transgressors and you too will be forgiven. Can you?" Cresasern continued saying weakly.

"You do believe it---?" Dave asked, more surprised than ever.

"My last hope," Cresasern whispered.

Dave simply shook his head as the Asian woman watched closely the interesting interaction occurring before her.

"Listen up, you! Your mother and father weren't at fault. Circumstances overpowered them, you got to let it go," Cresasern implored seriously, an overwhelming sadness evidently tingeing his feeble voice.

"How do you know?" Dave snapped back.

Before Cresasern could answer an orderly came into the room and told Dave he had an urgent phone call outside.

Thinking it must be Heda; Dave bade the troubled Cresasern rest and wait a bit until he returned momentarily.

Dave followed the fellow and soon stood before the reception desk's video phone.

The face in the screen staring back at Dave wasn't Heda's but to his surprise; the twisted wild, contorted one of Clive Waddell.

"I have your girlfriend here! I'm gonna feed her to that tornado thing this very night! If you want to watch, take the A-1 out to Bright Gate abbey! Come alone, right now!" Clive shouted shrilly.

Dave could see Heda struggling in the background behind Clive in a fast moving car and his heart and pulse pounded in fear.

"You're a dead man!" Dave snarled as the line suddenly went dead.

"Want some company?" Bruno asked.

Chapter 12

Monday, October 24, 2016

Bright Gate's ancient medieval grey stone turrets could just be seen in the distance jutting out before the setting Sun's last golden rays. The two jetted, oval, sky cab sped fast over rolling hills and green valleys following the A-1 highway north toward that old castle nestled high and snugly on the wooded outskirts, below Harpenden.

Dave was beside himself with fear and dread while Bruno sat close nervously checking his automatic laser pistol again and again. Dave felt positively naked without a weapon, but Cresasern advised that it was better to go without, though Dave wasn't so sure. The Hackney pilot was as good as they come and he held the sky cab steady and level and as low as possible to avoid detection.

Many troubling thoughts ran through Dave's mind this dark evening as he valiantly strove mightily to think this thing through calmly and rationally in order to save Heda and to make some sense of all the troubling but enlightening information Cresasern told him earlier. For somehow, some way; Dave knew deep in his soul that Cresasern had given him the very thing he sought; the useful key to winning this fight. Problem was how to find it, Dave wondered.

As the sky cab came down slowly for its landing, Dave and Bruno saw the abbey's large oaken front doors were splintered and smashed in and they feared the worst.

Gaining the entrance they saw wreckage here and there and a prone, still, long robed monk or two.

It was Bruno who heard it first! A sound of men's heated angry shouting emanated from much deeper in the abbey and Dave and Bruno followed it.

Soon they both stood at the entrance to the abbey's great hall and saw the crowd arrayed before them. Heda stood held tightly, under pointed guns, struggling as best she could, between two armed guards, the other three flanked them, while Clive paced to and fro behind them all ranting away to himself, it appeared. A single monk lay apparently dead behind Clive.

Heda and Dave locked eyes in quiet despair.

Bruno and Dave then rushed into the room to the utter amusement of those awaiting them in there.

"I said alone!" Clive shouted shrilly as he hefted his Luger machine pistol and shooting close between his own guards to their dismay, shot the rushing Bruno.

Bruno grabbed his chest and fell in a heap back on the floor in front but away to the side of Clive's shaken up crew before him.

Clive now leveled the Luger pistol dead on at Dave's head and shouted, "Stop! Best wait a bit sport; I'd hate to kill you too soon. I think we have company!"

Dave stopped in his tracks as all in the room stood still and listened to that dreaded sound that signaled something awful nearing that some knew was coming and others didn't.

"Grab him! Place him here in front of us, next to the girl! Quick!" Clive ordered his three flanking guards who complied as fast as they nervously could under the circumstances.

Thus Dave and Heda found themselves bound by strong hands, with guns at their heads, with that threatening sound growing nearer and louder by the second.

The loud, frightening sound of the rushing tornado grew louder as it came closer. Then they saw it! It came boldly rushing in the door that Dave and Bruno had just come in.

The doorway then filled up with the sight of the whirling twenty foot tall tornado twisting this way and that churning up furniture and other bits of nearby loose debris in a twisting mass of destruction.

Suddenly the tornado rushed into the room right at the startled mass of people before it with a rush as Clive screamed, "Stop or I'll kill them---!"

The tornado, seemingly in answer, abruptly stopped some four feet away from the shaking band of people and started to slow its spin. Its spinning decreased slowly until it finally swirled away and before the surprised people finally stood the form of a large man.

As the large gray swirling cloud further dissipated all saw all too well who it was.

"It boomed, "Go ahead! I'd like that!"

Dave and Heda, being in the forefront, first confronted the thing and couldn't believe their eyes as to what they were seeing, recognizing it for what they thought it was. The guards holding them began to visibly shake and quake in their boots as they slowly realized what big trouble they were in.

"You can't pass through them! I know all about you!" Clive shouted nervously, looking to his guards sheepishly for support. They looked back in ignorant surprise.

The thing laughed a resounding laugh that shook the building's very foundations.

"You don't know jack shit, super man!" it boomed as a long, thick, shiny wickedly curved sword suddenly appeared and started to steadily grow ever longer out of its left hand.

With that the thing seemed to disappear, right before their stunned eyes; at least that was what all saw, or thought they saw.

"What's this?" Clive asked even as he somehow inexpiably felt something sinister appear out of thin air behind him.

The thing grabbed him from behind and with that the two closest guards holding Dave and Heda both wisely bolted fast towards the door from whence the thing had so recently come.

Suddenly loose, Dave and Heda rushed to escape, Dave stopping to pick up Bruno. As he hefted the big man Dave glanced back to see the titanic struggle enfolding behind him. Somehow he knew it would be a short one.

The creature was keeping its human form as it attacked Clive and the three remaining guards. Clive wielded his blade and immense super human strength as well as he could but soon the creature was happily shredding them all amid useless gunfire and many harrowing screams on their part and with many shouts of hellish glee on the creatures' part.

Hefting the limp, moaning Bruno proved pointless as Dave and Heda could only barely get the big wounded man over to the far wall as the grisly fight before them finally came to its logical conclusion. With his last plaintive cry in this world, Clive, hoisted high; impaled and transfixed by the creature's shining scimitar of a blade signaled the end of the conflict.

Finished, the creature now turned and approached Dave, Heda, and the unconscious Bruno with its sinister blade growing longer anew.

Heda was ready to bolt and would have but Dave restrained her soothingly with, "there's no running from that thing! Trust me---Please! Rid your heart of any and all hate and resentment! Pray! Pray like you never prayed before! I'll take it on first, if I go down---you run!"

Heda, against her better fearful judgment, meekly complied and took his hand and rose with him to face this frightening whatever.

Dave faced the creature as it approached and abruptly stopped four feet away, glowering at them with its frighteningly knowing red eyes. It still retained the form of the man but it was now grotesquely covered in dark blood.

To say that Dave and Heda were experiencing the most fearful time of their lives right now would be a gross understatement. Heda's nails dug deep into his jacket and would have drawn blood if not for the leather separating his arm, but Dave didn't feel any of it; so engrossed as he was in praying and remembering Cresasern's instructions.

"Were you....?" Heda began but was stopped by the overpowering stench emanating from the creature.

"No! Luckily for you I found this open one after you did!" the creature snarled.

Dave now felt the very air, heating up before him; pushing back against him in thick ripples of force as the creature seemed to try shoving itself forward to no avail. Somehow, happily, his crucifix found its way into his clenched fist.

Dave remembered now something included in Cresasern's safe's notes and reckoned that the creature was probably lying to Heda. An admonition shouted in Dave's head to the effect: "Woe unto he who trusts the veracity of a demon from hell!"

Dave thus knew they faced a minor evil entity; one who could infest a host for sure, but the evil thing was limited and still had to do its own dirty work; the sure sign of a less powerful whatever it is. This one couldn't cause wars or famines or such other calamities that the powerful ones could but it had been and was still a big bother to anyone in its way.

The creature snarled again at the two shivering people before it.

"It's over! You got what you came after!" Dave stated plainly, strongly.

Heda violently shivered anew beside him all too strongly for his present liking.

"Clive cheated me out of one; Morgan, the grunt!" It railed loudly, shaking the building.

"No matter, you can't hurt us! We didn't willingly thwart your quest!" Dave shouted back bravely.

"Don't believe everything that sinner Cresasern tells you! He still can't get his nerve up to tell you that he's your father, the one that abandoned you!" the creature shouted accusatorily.

"I know! I forgive him!" Dave answered plainly, surprising himself greatly with this calming realization.

"Why?" Heda suddenly asked the creature as her courage slowly built up in her.

Dave wasn't sure what she meant exactly but the creature did.

"I don't suffer at all humans usurping, mocking me, or my works! They, the ones I killed, called to me in Havana---loudly!" the creature snarled back, blithely, lazily, licking blood from its long curved blade with its long red tongue.

Dave and Heda visibly shook at this sight.

"Do you actually think that a faux Moslem sinner and a faux Christian sinner from totally opposite sides of this planet can come together and stop me?" the creature laughed loudly.

"Yes---! We're the beginning of those who have, with GOD's grace, are beginning to outgrow you and your evil influences, and there's more of us being born everyday!" Dave barked happily.

The creature wavered and shimmered violently, again pushing against something Dave and Heda couldn't see, but felt the effects very strongly, and were very glad stood mightily between them and that unknown creature's evil.

"I'll see you again! Soon!" the creature loudly threatened, while its blade receded into nothingness and it began to whirl about anew and soon it violently whirled itself out of the building to the abject relief of the living inside.

"I know!" Dave said after the creature had left.

~~~~~

Albion lazily sauntered about closing up the house. Locking the locks and putting out the lights so much later after his missed midnight tea as was his usual custom gave him a much needed sense of order in his new life.

The cat, Miss Sidney by name, a fat yellow ringed tabby, regarded him warily with her shining green eyes as he rudely encroached on her usual late night time vigils.

Noticing the phone blinking he knew there was a message waiting.

It had been a very busy night, this last time out at Bright Gate abbey, once again cleaning up and counting the tornado shredded bodies earlier this night. Happily now he had reason to and hoped that was the last of that.

"Oh well what the hell," he figured, retrieving the message against his better policeman's instincts.

The voice shook, quaked, and squeaked as well as he remembered it could.

"Egon, dear, I made a big mistake! I've been such a fool. Pick up I want you to---."

With that Albion terminated the expected message not wishing to hear the rest this night.

"Egon! Are you coming back to bed?" this request suddenly came from the bedroom.

"Certainly honey!" Albion responded quickly as he skipped on down the hallway toward what he now referred to as his "pleasure room". Besides, it wouldn't do, he knew, to keep the amply endowed, always voracious Officer Iris Muldoon waiting too long, that is if he wanted to miss out on more pleasure in one night than he'd gotten during thirty years with Florence.

~~~~~

Tuesday, November 8, 2016

Dave had to admit it; Bruno looked good, you'd never suspect that he'd been shot a fortnight ago. The burly fellow was smiling and happily joking as never before, perhaps they glued and fixed him up too well, Dave wondered humorously.

Things were going well; Heda surprisingly agreed to marry him! The Ripper killings had stopped as suddenly as they began! Cresasern was recovering and had worked up the courage to tell Dave how he and Dave's young mother had dropped the ball regarding him so many lost years ago. She had been too young and troubled to keep Dave and so had left him on the park bench prior to her suicide without informing Cresasern about the birth. He just learned that Dave was his son a scant year ago from an angry relative of the mother.

While in the confessing mode; Cresasern also admitted to tracking his son and pressuring Image Retrieval to give Dave a job and this London assignment in particular. It hadn't been easy, but forgiveness, the giving and the getting, now pervaded Dave's life as never before and he knew he was the better off for it.

The three friends were standing in the middle of the airport's "hub". The hub was the round area assembly area in the middle of the airport from which radiated the many spokes or tramways which led to the various routes to the overseas terminals here at New Heathrow.

Bruno was off to Alexandria Egypt while Dave and Heda were heading for Pakistan for their nuptials.

"Take care of yourself," Heda told Bruno.

"Wish I was going with you two," Bruno joked with a wicked wink, not wanting to outwardly express his concern about his mission to Alexandria. Powerful forces were at work there to thwart the collection of long lost human knowledge. Bruno knew this wouldn't be a cake walk.

"Not a chance!" Dave retorted quickly hugging Heda close.

Overhead the news ticker spelled out: "Fifteen days since Jack's last Ripping, London breathing much easier!....Fires consume almost a third of Marseilles in Moslem induced rioting!....North Korea strikes back at China with missile attacks!....One Jupiter rocket still firing as doomed space station enters Sun's gravitational field!.....Cancer cured with cloned anti-viral antibody injections--- so speculated by AMA!"

The human airport announcer suddenly reported via loudspeaker that Bruno's jump jet was boarding now so he and Dave and Heda bid farewell for now.

"Dave, there's something I have to tell you!" Heda said seriously, thinking how awkward it would be if he first heard about Clive from her family.

"No there isn't! Unless it's to say you don't love me anymore," Dave simply responded, and with a wink, "I know everything else I need to know!"

Heda smiled now the smile that warmed his heart and curled his toes.

Dave and Heda thus went locked hand in hand back up the hub toward their flight entrance when she saw it first.

"Look!" Heda shouted, grasping Dave's hand hard.

Dave watched in rapt disbelief as the creature came striding regally up the hub from the opposite direction.

Dave and Heda stopped in their tracks as it approached and soon stood it before them, happily to them, observing its usual four foot cushion.

Overhead, three curious buzzer security drones dipped once above near the creature then scurried away awful fast.

The imposing creature now standing before them was in stark contrast to its appearance last time in the abbey. Gone were their tattered clothes all awash in blood, to be replaced this fine sparkling English morning with a beautifully tailored tan suit, over which it sported a fashionable tartan cape. On its head sitting as rakish as possible was a tan Tyrolean fur hat. Prominently; out of the creature's overly wide mouth blatantly dangled an obscenely expensive Havana cigar. The creature's skin positively glowed a rich gold, indicative of its wealth and position. A monocle over its left eye lent it an air of utter sophisticated elegance that Dave and Heda knew was totally false.

The creature now looked so much like the part it was so brazenly and aptly playing this day that it would easily fool anyone who had known it before it was the creature.

It brazenly, leering evilly away, pirouetted once around before them with arms extended outward and cape a twirl over dramatically and braved, "I clean up well, don't you think?"

Dave and Heda stepped back a pace.

"Smart move!" Alberto Arethusa Harvernera loudly laughed.

"We're not afraid of you!" Heda shouted, grabbing Dave's arm hard again.

Dave marveled at the man creature before them; it now falsely represented the very essence of the Hollywood star. Pressed hair, expensive clothes, shining eyes and skin, haughty attitude, sneering visage, obtuse monocle, and manicured nails, all served to exhibit that which all now accepted as a successful American movie star.

"Liars! You sure are!" Harvernera snidely snapped.

"No, no we aren't!" Dave bravely shouted as he stepped forward a pace toward the august appearing creature.

Harvernera now back stepped a pace, but kept his evil eyes dead on the two before him.

Noticing the creature's reaction, Dave knew deep down in his soul that one day, when he was stronger, wiser, he would definitely make a serious move against the creature.

"I'll be waiting!" Harvernera responded ominously, "I'm off now to D.C. then Hollywood for my comeback. I have many bones to pick with many windbags who mock me still! Seek me where you read about me!"

Dave fumed inwardly, realizing that that disgusting thing could read his thoughts faster and easier than he could think them up.

With that final warning, Harvernera haughtily passed by them with a flourish of his cape and went on toward the U.S. flights terminal striding regally with all the airs of bravado and panache he could muster, like the celebrated movie star that he was once.

Turning, but warily watching their backs, as the creature disappeared up the ramp, Dave and Heda once again joined hands and walked up the tram toward their plane, Dave feeling better and better the further away he felt that creature was from him.

Their new happy life beckoned and Dave had a lot to look forward to, for the first time in his life. He now would have a loving, beautiful wife and a rich father, albeit a latecomer, and as Heda had often warned; a doting mother-in-law, he soberly remembered.

Yes Dave had a lot to look forward to; also Cresasern wanted to replace the biological Extraminator behind his left eye with a new and improved model when they returned. The newly included improvement Cresasern had mentioned made Dave's mind and heart race fast with interest and curiosity. Dave could eagerly remember what his father seriously stated so simply but with so much impact.

He had said, "Sound!"

The End